THE
SECOND CHANCE
OF BENJAMIN
WATERFALLS

THE
SECOND CHANCE
OF BENJAMIN
WATERFALLS

JAMES BIRD

Feiwel and Friends
New York

A Feiwel and Friends Book
An imprint of Macmillan Publishing Group, LLC
120 Broadway, New York, NY 10271
mackids.com

Our books may be purchased in bulk for promotional, educational, or
business use. Please contact your local bookseller or the Macmillan Corporate
and Premium Sales Department at (800) 221-7945 ext. 5442 or by email at
MacmillanSpecialMarkets@macmillan.com.

Library of Congress Cataloging-in-Publication Data is available.

First edition, 2022
Interior design by Angela Jun

Printed in the United States of America by LSC Communications,
Harrisonburg, Virginia

Feiwel and Friends logo designed by Filomena Tuosto

ISBN 978-1-250-81156-1 (hardcover)
1 3 5 7 9 10 8 6 4 2

Boozhoo! This story is dedicated to all my friends
and relatives of the Grand Portage (Gitchi Onigaming)
Ojibwe. I hope I make you as proud of me as
I am proud of you. And to my soulmate Adriana Mather,
and my shining son, Wolf (Ma'iingan).

———————————

Your life will become better by making other lives better.
—*Will Smith*

CHAPTER 1

MAKWA (BEAR)

I don't know why I stole it. I don't have any younger siblings or cousins that would have wanted it. It's not like I know any *kids* I'd give it to. But still, I saw the stuffed bear on the department store shelf and grabbed it. And as soon as I walked out, I was met by security. Maybe I should have just paid for it. It was only twenty bucks.

Instead, I ran. And no more than ten steps into the parking lot, I was tackled and pinned to the asphalt until the police arrived. It would be funny if it wasn't so confusing. A stuffed bear? It makes no sense at all.

This happened five days ago. My mom hasn't said much to me since, other than telling me to go to school each morning. We're not exactly close anymore, but she usually doesn't stop trying to get through to me when I mess up, which according to her, is quite often.

This time, however, I can tell by her hunched shoulders that she is quietly defeated. I've never intentionally done anything bad to her. I steal things, big deal. It has nothing to do with her. I mean, I'm thirteen years old. This is what I'm supposed to do, right? All my friends do bad things.

My mom shouldn't worry about me so much. She has enough on her mind. Like rent, bills, work, food, and somehow trying to find time to sleep in between all of that stuff.

Life for us hasn't been easy. But she's always said she's happy because she has me.

Right now, she looks anything but happy. She is staring straight ahead, avoiding having to look at me. I know she feels my eyes on her, though, by the way she shifts her body the longer I glare at her. Truth is, I do feel bad for putting her through this.

It's like every time I get in trouble, it somehow adds years to her body. Every trip to the principal's office or a courtroom adds wrinkles around her eyes. Her straight long hair is now more silver than black, her eyes are now heavier and redder rather than round and brown, and her smile has faded, leaving riverbeds around her lips. But today, she's in a red dress under a black blazer. I haven't seen her this formal in years. I guess my sentencing is a reason to dress up.

I watch her shift and cross her legs. Most people find these wooden benches uncomfortable, but not me; I'm kind of used to them by now. This is my sixth time in a courtroom. I guess that's not something to brag about, but my mama always says, *Be proud of what you're good at*, and I must say, I'm pretty darn good at taking things that aren't mine. Or at least I thought I was.

"Case 83-212. Let's see . . . Benjamin Waterfalls, please stand," the judge says from his bench, after reading my file, which has gotten thicker with each visit.

I've had this judge once before. He's one of the nicer ones. He gave me a warning last time and made me promise I'd never be in front of him again, but I'm sure that's what a lot of judges say to screwups like me. Besides, if everyone kept that promise, he'd be out of a job. So technically, he should thank me for stealing. But I doubt he'll see it that way.

The black and gold placard on his bench reads HONOR-ABLE JUDGE Z. MASON. Last time I was here, I wondered what his first name was. Zeke? Zachary? Zander? Zane? Zion? I don't know, Zeus? But more than wanting to know his name, I fantasized about stealing that fancy placard from right under his nose. I bet I wouldn't get much for it, but still . . . It would be a fun little trophy for my room.

I stand, and as soon as I do, my mother rises to her feet to join me.

"Benjamin. Back again . . ." Judge Mason says this like his courthouse is a roller coaster that I just can't get enough of riding. The moment I get off, I run back to the line, cut

3

to the front, and hop back on again. "I remember last time you were here, you made me a promise. That promise is now broken. Tell me, why do you keep stealing?" he asks.

"Not everyone gets paid to sit up there, judging people all day," I say, which immediately is followed by a disappointed sigh from my mom.

"I see you still think this is all a big joke," Judge Mason continues as he reads from my file. "Well, let's see what you've been up to, shall we . . . Fighting, shoplifting, shoplifting, vandalizing property, shoplifting, and what brings you in this time . . . Interesting, more shoplifting."

"I like to stay busy," I say.

"Benny! Enough!" Mom snaps.

"And I see you brought your mother with you this time." Mason looks up from my paperwork. "We meet at last, Mrs. Waterfalls."

"*Miss* Waterfalls, Your Honor. And yes, at last . . . However, I wish it were under different circumstances."

"As do I. Your son has a knack for getting into trouble. I know you are here to support him, but I'm afraid, with Benjamin, I have completely run out of leniency."

"I am here to make sure you show zero leniency, Your Honor," she says.

"Mom?" I blurt out, but she avoids my eyes. What is she doing? She's supposed to be on my side.

"That's good to hear," the judge continues. "Sometimes, the hard road is the only one left for these kids to take."

"Give him your worst," my mother says, still not meeting my eyes. "He's a tough guy, or so he thinks."

"Mom!"

"Well, let's just see how tough he is," the judge says in a tone that reminds me of a game show host who's about to reveal what's behind door number three.

What is going on? Why are they teaming up against me? So, I shoplifted a few times and got into a few fights, so what?

"Your Honor, my mom is just really upset right now. I wouldn't take her words too seriously," I argue, since my own mother won't speak up for me.

"Perhaps you should have taken her words, and mine, a bit more seriously, young man. We could have avoided this altogether, but here we are," Mason says, and pushes his palms together like he just washed his hands. What does that mean? Does that make me the dirt he just rinsed away from his skin? I get the feeling that I've ridden this roller coaster for the very last time.

I feel so betrayed. My own mother is selling me out. My own flesh and blood marching me straight to the guillotine. What happened to a mother's love being unconditional?

Judge Mason clears his throat. "Benjamin Waterfalls. You have displayed an unfortunate pattern that only leads to a future behind bars. If I do nothing, nothing will change. Thus, it is my decision to place you in a juvenile detention center for no less than sixty days, after which, you will be on a twelve-month probation period, where you will be assigned to complete no less than two hundred and fifty hours of community service."

"What? Wait. That's going to ruin my life," I blurt out.

"Or save it," the judge fires back.

This can't be happening. "Mom! Do something. I can't be caged like some animal," I plead.

She finally turns to me. I can see in her eyes that even she feels the punishment is a bit harsh.

"Your Honor," she says, "as fitting and deserving as your punishment sounds, may I offer up an alternative solution? One that I feel may be more effective?"

The judge looks curious. He leans back into his chair and rubs his chin. "The floor is yours, however, if this is about grounding him by keeping him home all day, then I don't believe it is going to help," he says.

What is her angle? Is she coming to my rescue, or is she making everything worse? I can't tell. She turned away from me again.

"What I am proposing is actually the opposite of keeping him home, Your Honor," she says.

"I'll admit, I am intrigued. Please continue," he says.

What is she talking about? I get nervous as my mom clears her throat and squares her shoulders, about to deliver her idea of how best to punish me. "I suggest sending him to temporarily live with his father," she says.

My what? She just said the *F* word. The one word that

makes me all kinds of *F* words: furious, frustrated, and fuming. The man is a fake. He's a fraud. He's no father, he's a freaking failure.

"My father is dead!" I shout.

"I assure you, Judge, his father is not dead," she snaps back.

"He's dead to me," I say, turning my head to her.

"And how do you think this will help Benjamin?" the judge asks.

"Like my son, his father often took the wrong path to find his way home. He'd lie. He'd cheat. And yes—like father, like son—he'd steal. But I knew the real him. And he had a big heart. Unfortunately, he'd often fill his heart with alcohol. And sadly, our marriage drowned. I sent him away. I told him to search for the light that had left his eyes. This was seven years ago when Benny was six years old," she says, and sighs.

"I'm still failing to see how this will help your son." The judge rests his chin in his hand.

"You see, his father is a slow learner, Your Honor, but he never gave up. After years of searching, he has recently found his light. And although I lost a husband, I don't believe my son has lost his father. He needs his dad now. I look at my son, and I see the light in his eyes is gone. I spoke to his dad, and he has agreed to help his son find that light. It won't be easy. But as troubled as they both can be, I also see the same strength inside. He has a warrior's heart. Benny is smart. He is kind. He is a survivor. And if you agree to this request, my Benny will find the right path home," she says, her gaze fixed on the judge.

He stares back at my mother, tapping his fingers against the bench like a king on his throne.

"He returned to his roots. Think of it as a Native boot camp. My son will learn how to correct his path the original way . . . the Anishinaabe way," she says.

"I'm unfamiliar with Native boot camps. Are they—"

"They're not on the books. There is no agency. They are unofficial. But they are effective," my mom says in a lower tone, like she's revealing a secret.

"And you believe this unofficial boot camp will rehabilitate your son?" Mason leans toward her.

Really? He's buying into this?

"Your Honor, Benjamin is a thief. He's a liar. He has trouble written all over him. But one thing he is not is hopeless. I will not give up on my son. And it is his father's duty to teach him how to be not just a man, but a meno-izhiwebizid," she says. "A good man."

Oh Gawd. She's pulling out Ojibwe words. What is she up to?

"And where would this take place?" Mason asks.

"About three hours north. In Gichi-onigaming. Our first home, Grand Portage."

"Well . . . normally, I'd advise against family intervention outside of the law, but, as a fellow Duluth, Minnesotan once said, 'The times, they are a-changin'.'"

My mom smiles. "I do love me some Dylan wisdom," she says.

Judge Mason smiles back. I see an opening, and I have to take it. There's no way I'm going to live with my dad. I buried him seven years ago. I will stay here, in Duluth, even if it's behind bars.

"Mom. Judge, um, Your Honor. Let's make a deal. Let me take the community service hours. Probation is fine too. I've learned my lesson, but don't send me to stay with my dad. I don't want to see him. Please, don't do this," I beg.

My mother turns to me, looks me dead in the face. "Oh, Benny, I didn't do this. You did," she says, and turns back to the judge.

"Your Honor?" she asks.

Mason takes a deep breath. The seconds feel like hours. This is killing me. Why did I have to get the nice judge? A mean one would have just slapped his sentence down and would have been done with it. Why is this guy considering my mom's awful idea?

"I will allow it, but this is his final chance to turn it all around." Mason seems reluctant to look away from my mother, but he finally does. "If you end up back in my courtroom again, I won't be so accommodating. Is this understood?" he says.

"I'd expect nothing less," my mother replies. Is she serious?

"Wait!" I say, staring at my mom. "You really think some powwow is gonna clean me up? You think my dad has changed? No way. He might have fooled you, but people like him don't change."

"Do people like you change?" Mason asks me.

I look at him and want to say something clever, but "I don't know" is all I can offer.

"Well, let's find out," he says.

"Do I have a choice?" I ask. "Do I have any say in this?"

"No. You don't. You gave up that right when you stopped being a kid," he adds.

"I am a kid. Kids steal. Kids get in trouble. Just let me pay for it like everyone else. Please."

"No. Kids play basketball in the park. Kids read books. Kids go to the movies with their friends. They play video games and wear baggy pants and sometimes stay out late and get grounded. You're not behaving like a kid anymore. But I, like your mother here, am not one to easily throw in the towel. We're giving you one last shot, Benjamin. Make it count." Then Judge Mason slams down his gavel with the force of a basketball player slam-dunking the ball.

"Thank you, Your Honor," my mom says, smiling.

"Good luck with your son, Mrs. Waterfalls."

"Miss Waterfalls," she corrects him again.

They share another smile, which lasts a bit too long.

Ugh. Not only did they team up against me, but now they're making googly eyes at each other. Could today get worse?

"You want me to wait outside while you two exchange numbers?" I ask sarcastically, but my mother nods.

"Seriously?" I say, and look at the judge, who is also smiling.

Oh Gawd. This is awful. I walk toward the exit as my mom approaches the bench.

I push the doors open and enter the hallway. There are a lot of families standing around. I guess a lot of parents have bad apple seeds. I walk toward the doors that lead to the parking garage and realize this all happened because of that stuffed bear. I'm probably the dumbest thief to ever enter this courthouse.

CHAPTER 2

MAAZHI-GIIZHIGAD (IT IS A BAD DAY)

My mother and I are silent the entire drive home. What's left to say? She's getting rid of me, and I'm going to spend the next however many days-weeks-months with a guy that split seven years ago. The guy I looked up to until I realized who he really was.

We enter our apartment, and I make a beeline to my room. For living on the poor side of town, you'd never guess our struggle by the contents of my room. I have a stack of brand-new denim jeans, several unopened boxes of electronics, perfumes, colognes, and half a dozen wallets. All hidden under my bed.

I make most of my money stealing from the Miller Hill Mall and then I turn around and sell everything to kids at school for a fraction of the price. Sometimes, I even hit up the campuses of Denfeld and Central to sell the merchandise to high schoolers. Thieving is my job, and I take my job seriously. This is why my bedroom door is usually locked. Until now, I had the good fortune of having a mom who respects privacy. So, naturally, I've taken full advantage of that.

I slip my key into the door, but . . . oh crap, it's unlocked. She was in here. I swing the door open and dive to the floor near my bed. I lift my droopy Timberwolves comforter back and look under it. My jaw drops. Nothing. It's gone. All of it.

AHHH! I feel the blood inside of me begin to boil. Panic rolls out in beads of sweat. How could she do this to me?

"Mom!" I shout, but she's already standing behind me, arms crossed and looking smug.

"Where's all my stuff?" I ask.

"All *your* stuff?"

"My stuff! Where is it?" I repeat.

"Well, looks like someone broke in and took everything. Thieves really suck, don't they?" she says, and walks victoriously out of my room.

I slam my door shut so hard it rattles the walls. What did she do with all of it? Usually, whenever she catches me with a stolen wallet, she threatens to take it to the police station to drop it off. I guess she actually did it this time. She clearly doesn't care that I just lost out on customers, money, and street cred. But doesn't she realize that the money I slip into her purse at night, especially when rent is due, comes from all this stuff? Now what is she going to do?

"You're lucky I didn't call the police!" my mom shouts from the living room.

She's right. Knowing my mom could just sell me out the way she did to the judge, I am lucky she didn't have me arrested. That would have been a first-class ticket to juvenile hall.

Did she take off work and spend the day returning everything to each store while I was at school? Was she embarrassed to stand in line with the customers that were there to actually shop? Did I humiliate her? How did she explain it to everyone? Did she say, *My good-for-nothing son stole all this stuff from under your noses, and I'm here to give it back*?

I hope she doesn't get in trouble for missing work. She needs her job. She's worked so hard for it. She studied every night to get her certification and worked even harder to land a job at Duluth's best physical therapy facility. Years and years of dedicating her life to PT, all down the tubes because she had to clean up her son's mess. Ugh.

But if she does lose her job, she has no one to blame but herself. She did this. She stuck her nose where it didn't belong. She will have hurt herself by trying to hurt me.

I slide open a dresser drawer and see that even some of my clothes are gone. What? I turn to ask my mom where the heck my underwear went, but the answer is staring back at me near my bedroom door . . . A packed suitcase.

Oh yeah. I'm leaving.

I don't know how my mom knew the judge would agree to her request, but she somehow did, because the bus ticket on the suitcase is for early tomorrow morning. A two hour and forty-seven minute bus ride from Duluth to Grand Portage.

This sucks.

I don't remember much about Grand Portage. We've only gone back a couple times to bury distant relatives, when we were still a family. Those were long-ago times. But they're also some of my favorite memories as a kid, which is weird because technically we were always on our way to a funeral. But that's when my parents were happy. That's when they laughed. When my dad would play with me. When my mom would call us both goofballs.

But when Duluth's Savannah-Pacific plant closed and my dad, along with 144 other workers suddenly had no job, I suddenly had no dad. He changed so fast. It caught my mom and me completely off guard. His smile flipped over like a turtle and never really found a way back to its feet.

That was seven years ago. I was just a little rug rat that hung on to his leg when he walked. I don't even remember what he looks like. I mean, I kind of do, but people change. I look completely different now. Back then, I was a scrawny six-year-old kid that wanted to grow up and be exactly like my dad.

But when I picture him now, I don't see my hero. I see an angry man that yelled too loud and locked himself in his room all day. I see a guy who the cops would bring home in the middle of the night after he'd made a scene at the local bar. Some nights, my mom and I would drive around looking for him, only to find him hanging outside of the liquor store or begging for money at random gas stations. My mom was so embarrassed. I was too young to be embarrassed. I was just happy we found him. My mom tried to shelter me from what was really happening. She made it a game for us to play. First one to find Daddy wins.

Then he left for good.

When I realized that this was not a game that families play, I got angry. I guess that's when I started stealing. Not to be like him, but to show him I was better than him. He got caught. He was a lousy thief. I wanted to prove to him that I could do what he did, only better. At everything, even the things no one should be proud of. I'm really good at it too. I can steal the wings off a bee and not get caught. After a while, it just made sense to keep doing it. The more I took, the better I felt about being good at something.

But since getting busted for stealing that stupid stuffed bear, I'm starting to think that maybe I'm not so good after all, even though I stuck to my game plan. I have five rules for stealing. And I always follow my rules.

1. Count how many security guards there are between me and the exit.
2. Check for cameras.
3. Make sure I'm wearing baggy clothes that have deep pockets.
4. Have another item in my hand so when I pocket the item I want, I'm seen putting the decoy item back on the shelf.
5. And lastly, only steal what I know I can flip, which means turn around and sell.

I broke all my rules with that stuffed bear. I saw it, stopped, and stared at it for a good minute or two. It was like that bear was calling to me to take it home. I grabbed it and walked out of the store. And the award for Worst Thief Ever goes to . . . me.

I hear the shower run from down the hall. That's one advantage of being a thief and living in a small apartment: thin walls. I can hear everything. At times like right now, I know she's occupied, so I have a few minutes to sneak into her room, find her purse, and snake a few bucks. Now that she took all my stuff, I'm gonna need some money for this pointless trip she's sending me on. It's only fair.

I quietly open my door, tiptoe down the hall, and slip into her room. Her purse is on her bed. She's way too trusting; I mean, there are thieves everywhere. I open it and rifle through it. Where the heck is the cash? I dump the contents out onto the Thunderbird blanket her mom made before she died. Out fall keys, wallet, and about two bucks in change, but still, no dollar bills.

I feel three light taps on my shoulder. I turn around and see my mom standing there, at the doorway, with dripping wet hair and her body wrapped in a red towel. Clever. She kept the water running so I'd think I had more time.

"I'd assume that stealing from your own mother qualifies as hitting rock bottom, wouldn't you agree?" she says.

I shovel all her belongings back into her purse. "I'm sorry . . . But—"

"No buts. You've done many things I am very upset about, but right now, at this moment, I've never been more disappointed."

"I was only looking for—"

"Go to your room, Benny."

"I said I was sorry."

"I don't care if you're sorry. We have nothing without trust, and you just took ours away."

Ugh. I feel like crap. No, worse than crap. I feel like the crap that crap craps out: crap crap. She's right. There should be a line, even for me, and stealing from the woman who gave birth to you definitely crosses that line.

CHAPTER 3

GIMOODISHKI [HE STEALS]

STEAL: *to take the property of another without permission or right, especially by secret or by force.*

It gives me a rush. The blood-pumping thrill of whether I'll get caught or not. The way my heart races as I walk out of the store carrying as many items as I can and not having to pay for them. And before that stuffed bear incident, I was convinced the world had never seen a better thief, even though I'd been caught before. But all thieves get caught at some point, it comes with the job. If I was never caught, no one would even know I'm a thief. And we all know, no one's perfect. But it was almost magical how I'd walk in with nothing and come out with whatever I wanted. Like a magician pulling a rabbit out of his hat, I was that good.

But, clearly, it does come with a cost.

My mom says she doesn't know who I am anymore. She says she *cannot fathom* her sweet boy doing such awful things. I tell her that it's not a big deal. This is America. Everybody steals. This country was founded on theft. I make her so sad. That's the only part of stealing I don't like. Moms shouldn't be sad. They should be happy. They pushed a human out of their body. That must be painful and terrifying. Eternal happiness should be the reward for something like that. And maybe it is. Maybe I'm just ruining her chance to be happy. Just like how my dad ruined it for me.

Maybe sending me away to live with him is Mom's way of closing the chapter on their marriage for good. It makes sense. They are divorced. All his stuff is gone; all the photographs of him have disappeared. In fact, I'm the only reminder of him, and now I'll be gone too. I know she says it's only until I change, but what if she said that just to get me out of the door? What if it is forever? What if I never change, or worse, what if I never want to change? Truth be told, the only thing I regret is getting caught.

We're stuck in traffic on the way to the bus station, which is pretty common here in Duluth, with all the construction that's been going on. Duluth loves its bridges. Our city is famous for them. I've always found it strange that people travel from all over the world to drive over our bridges. The Aerial Lift Bridge even has a visitor shop. And the Blatnik Bridge, which I've been on a million times, made its way to be on postcards and T-shirts. It connects Minnesota to Wisconsin. So my friends and I call it the Minnesconsin Bridge. Why am I thinking about bridges again? Oh, yeah, because my dad will assume his seven-year absence will just be water under the bridge between us. Fat chance. He burned that bridge the day he skipped out on me.

Mom will be late for work if we don't get to the bus soon. And with taking yesterday off to accompany me to court, I can tell she's worried.

I guess she's been worried since I was ten. That's when I started hanging out with the older kids from our neighborhood, who she calls the dropouts. I don't defend them because she's right, they are dropouts. I promised her I wouldn't end up like them. I'll be the first to admit that they're losers. But a good thing about hanging out with losers is that they don't judge you like other people do. It feels good not being judged. If I steal, it's nobody's business but mine . . . Well, and the sucker who I stole from.

I remember the moment my relationship with my mom fell apart. It was the first time I lied to her. Nothing has been the same since that night. It wasn't even a big lie. But it meant the earth to her. I stole a wallet, and when she saw it in my room, I told her I found it. She was so happy that I picked it up so we could return it to its owner. When I hesitated, she knew something was up. That was the pebble hitting the windshield of her heart.

In the end, my mom returned the wallet, and apparently the owner described in pretty good detail what the kid who stole it off a convenience store counter looked like. And my mom says her heart cracked then, and it has been slowly and steadily cracking ever since. After that night, we basically became two people living under one roof, not mother and son.

I guess she thinks that if I don't go live with my dad, I'll keep stealing, and sooner or later, her cracked heart will ultimately shatter. She tried her best. She taught me everything a dad was supposed to teach his son. How to throw a ball. How to catch. How to throw a punch. How to ride a bike. Math. Spelling. She even taught me how to change a tire. I'm not sure why I am being bombarded with all these memories right now. Maybe this happens to everyone right before they say their goodbyes?

"Can I ask you something? Or are you too mad to hear my voice?" I say as the traffic begins to finally move forward.

"What is it?" she says, keeping her eyes on the road.

"Was he a kleptomaniac?"

She turns to me, and I see a sparkle in her eyes, as if she is either about to cry or laugh. Is she driving down memory lane too? Or maybe she's just impressed I know what a kleptomaniac is. After all, it's a pretty big word, and I haven't really been doing so well in school lately.

"He would lie like a rug and cheat like a sailor, but as hard as he tried, he was never too good at stealing," she says.

"Really?" I say.

"He'd get caught stealing sand from a desert," she adds.

For some strange reason, I feel better knowing my particular set of skills is something I acquired on my own. I'd hate to give credit to the person who tore our family apart, who I refuse to let crawl back into my heart. Come to think of it, in a way, this is all his fault. He is why my mom had to pick up extra shifts. He's why I never got to spend enough time with her. And he is why my mom is always so sad now.

I know I'm contributing to it, but it's because of him that this is happening . . . And now he's the one to fix me? Mark my words: He will only make things worse. He ruins everything. It's the only thing he's good at.

But he wasn't always the destroyer of happiness. After all, my mom loved him once. And as hard as I try to deny it, so did I. That's why I hate him so much. He had everything and threw it all away. I wonder if, somewhere deep down in my mom's busted-up heart, she still loves him? I know I don't. I refuse to.

"He must have been decent at it. I mean, he stole your heart," I say, trying to make her smile in an attempt to salvage this car ride.

"I gave it to him. But he didn't take care of it, so I took it back," she says, and stiffens her face the same way she does when she's cutting onions in the kitchen and is trying with all her might to not cry because she just put her makeup on.

"Like me?"

"Like you what?" she asks.

"Like how I was good but turned bad, so now you're getting rid of me," I say.

"Benny, I'm not getting rid of you. I tried to fix whatever it is that is broken inside of you, but I couldn't. So I'm asking for help, that's all," she says.

"But he's probably the reason why I am how I am," I say.

"You are not him. You are you. Don't blame other people for who you are. That's the sign of a weak person. And you are many things, but weak is not one of them," she says.

"So, you think he and a bunch of old Indians are going to make me a better person?" I ask.

She laughs. "You've seen too many Westerns. Grand Portage is a wonderful place full of wonderful people," she says.

"Well, if it's so wonderful, why'd you leave?"

"We left because your father got a good job at the plant here in Duluth," she says.

"Well, that didn't last. It shut down. So why didn't we move again?"

"Because he's there now," she fires back.

"So what? Isn't he all rehabilitated? Or was that a lie?"

"He is. But he has his own life there . . . And we have our life here."

We finally pull up alongside the curb, directly under the

bus station's drop-off-zone sign. The car idles as she gets out and walks toward my side. I step out, grab my suitcase, and meet her on the curb. I don't know what awaits me in Grand Portage, so if this ends up being the last time I see or talk to my mom, I might as well show her that I'm not completely rotten to the core. My heart still works even though I haven't used it in a while.

"I'm sorry for not being who you want me to be," I say, and hug her.

She tightens her grip around my rib cage and leans into my ear. "You don't even know who you are yet, Benny. But this trip will reveal that to you. I promise you that," she whispers.

As I pull away, I see her quickly wipe tears from her eyes.

"I love you," she says, kisses my forehead, and walks back to the car.

She gets in and rolls down her window for her parting words: "Benny, remember to talk to strangers. It's literally the only way to make friends."

Up until ten years old, it was a rule to never talk to strangers, then one day it completely changed. Talk to everyone, make friends, help old people cross the street. Rules are weird like that. When one parent leaves, some of those rules get reversed. Like, when I was younger, my mom and dad would always say, "No more talking. It's bedtime. Go to sleep." But after he left, sometimes my mom would wake me up in the middle of the night after she got home from work and ask if I wanted to talk or do a puzzle. My favorite was when she'd let me skip school when she was lucky enough to have a day off. We'd play fart in the park. That's when we'd both eat a ton of ice cream, go to the park, and see who could make the loudest fart. She'd always win because she was lactose intolerant. But she'd still eat it because I loved ice cream so much.

I watch my mom drive away in a hurry. She's already late. I wonder if I'll ever see her again. Maybe that's a bit dramatic, but life has suddenly become unpredictable. A few days ago, I would have never imagined I'd be where I am now.

I pass through security and see a golden scarf in the tray next to mine. I don't particularly like gold, but other people do. People with money. Before I can even think about whether I should steal it, I'm already following my five rules. The security guards are busy helping old people up the ramps, the security cameras are facing in the direction of the buses, I am wearing a hoodie with deep pockets; I casually pick the scarf up and mix it with my stuff, stuffing it into my backpack before the owner returns from wherever he or she is, and the last rule, yeah, I can sell this scarf. It looks expensive. I'd get an easy twenty bucks for it, but like Duluth, Grand Portage is also right on Lake Superior. And it's farther north. It will be much colder. I may need it.

A soon as I zip up my backpack, a woman returns and gets the remaining contents out of her tray. She must be in a rush because she hasn't yet noticed her scarf is missing. Well, she must have not liked it too much if she doesn't realize it's gone. She throws on a jacket and zips it all the way up to her chin, completely covering her neck. Seriously? She didn't even need a scarf.

I swipe a bag of chips as I walk by one of the crowded food kiosks and reach my bus. I leave my suitcase with the pile of luggage beside it and hand the man my ticket. He rips it in half as I step inside. Ugh, it smells like cheese in here.

I take a seat near the back and lean my head against the window. The bus starts filling up with people, mixing the aroma. I smell cheese, perfume, and cigarettes, which turns my stomach. My dad started smoking when he lost his job. I've hated the smell ever since. Even when my friends would nick cigarettes from their parents and smoke them in the park, I didn't join in. They'd reek for the rest of the day. They smelled like my dad.

I just want to sleep. I woke up way too early this morning. I focus on the trees as the bus pulls away from the station. Since my mom took all my stuff, I have no music or video games to play. Now I'm going to have to listen to the two little kids in back of me argue over which is the coolest dinosaur ever the entire time, or I can listen to the teenage girl in front of me yapping away on her phone, explaining to one of her bestest best friends how her boyfriend is a loser for kissing that stuck-up rich girl at last night's party. This is hell, and I'm only two minutes into my trip.

I can tough it out. This ride may feel like weeks and smell like months, but it's only a few hours, and like my mom said, I'm many things, but I am not weak. I'm as strong as this smell.

CHAPTER 4

IMBAABAA [MY DAD]

I wake up to the sound of shuffling feet exiting the bus. I never wait in lines, so I sit and wait until I'm the last person off the bus. I do this because sometimes people forget things in their seat when traveling, so I eye-sweep every row as I make my way forward, looking for something to take. But other than a few crackers, a couple empty pop cans, and a magazine, there's nothing to grab. Oh, and the consensus was that the velociraptor was the coolest dinosaur ever.

Through the windows, the bus terminal in Grand Portage doesn't look too different from Duluth's. But as soon as I step off the bus, I can see, smell, hear, and feel the difference. Duluth is a city. Buildings everywhere, steel bridges, people bustling about, and cars racing by in all directions. But this place is filled with other things. The concrete and high-rises are replaced by large trees, and the steady flow of city cars and traffic is replaced by pickup trucks and motorcycles. This place is so green. Even the people walking around are in shades of green. I've never seen so many camouflage pants. And what's with all the plaid? A three-hour trip has taken me to another planet. A lush planet where people try to blend in with their surroundings. There must only be one store here, where the first floor is all plaid shirts and the second floor is all camouflage pants.

At least it smells good here, like trees and flowers. It's nice to not be smelling cheese anymore.

In between the breaks of green, I see blue. I even hear blue. I collect my suitcase and walk up a small, dirt-paved hill toward the bus station pickup zone and see the ocean. Technically, I know it's not an ocean, but this body of water stretches past the horizon and looks like it goes on forever. Lake Superior. I never really thought about how huge this lake is. It actually touches Duluth. I used to play in it when I was a kid. I guess someone could walk along the shore from Duluth to Grand Portage if they really wanted to. Good to know. If this place sucks major balls, I'll know how to get home. It may take a while, but—

"Benny?" a voice snaps me from my thoughts.

I turn around and see a tall man wearing a red plaid shirt, jeans, and a black newsboy cap staring at me. I recognize his eyes immediately. I knew those eyes when I was young, before depression glazed them over. I don't know what to say, so I smile. Obviously, he doesn't deserve a smile, but I have to do something.

He looks younger than I remember, even though he's seven years older now. His hair is much longer and darker than I imagined it would be. I don't know why I'd imagined him being a mostly bald, wrinkled up, bloated man now. I was way off. In fact, he looks fit and healthy. But he also looks nervous. He keeps rubbing his hands together and nodding his head.

"It's like she goes on forever, right?" he says, and slowly approaches me.

"Who?" I ask.

"Gichigami," he says, and points behind me.

I turn back to Lake Superior. With the sun's reflection, it's difficult to know which is the lake and which is the sky. Where one ends and one begins. The blues blend together blue-tifully.

"It's just a lake. I've seen it a million times," I say, and look down at my feet.

I stare at my shoes and try to remember how awful he is. My shoes are dirty. Dirty is bad. *Bad* rhymes with *dad*. Dad is bad. Right foot, left foot. Oh, that's right. Left. Dad left us. Now I remember. He threw his family away. I hate him.

"Yeah, but still, I'm in awe every time I see her," he says and is now inches away from me. Even our shadows are touching. I step back to separate them. I don't want us to touch at all.

"I remember taking you down to her. You'd play in the water for hours," he says. "You called the water Sun Blue. I've always liked that. Do you remember?"

"I was a kid. I'm not a kid anymore," I say.

"Yeah, I've heard."

"What did you hear?" I ask.

"Your mother said enough. But let's get you home. It's cold out here," he says.

"It's your home, not mine. And just so you know, I chose juvie, fines, and community service over coming here. This is all Mom's doing," I say, and walk off toward the parking lot.

I can't tell if he responds. The wind is picking up, drowning out most sounds. But I do hear his footsteps behind me. Following me. I slow down so he passes me up. I don't know where he parked or what car he drives. When he left, my mom kept the only car we had. He took the bus here back then, just as I took the bus here now.

As he passes me, he takes my suitcase from my hands. It happens so quickly that I don't have a chance to fight it. I hope he doesn't think I appreciate it, because I don't. It's just too late to get it back because we've reached his car. It's an old Jeep. The kind that used to pass us as we took our walks and he'd hit me on the arm and say, "Beep Beep Jeep!"

And now he owns one. I wonder if he bought it because he missed playing the game with me. I wonder where he got the money for it. It's old and beat up a bit, so I'm sure he bought it used, but still, Jeeps were our thing. Beep Beep Jeep was ours. Now it's his.

He tosses my suitcase in the back and opens my door.

"Stop trying to be nice. I know how to open doors," I say, which makes him laugh, which makes me more upset.

And I'm not saying thank you. He could carry a million suitcases and open a million doors, but I'll never thank this guy. Not in a million years.

"How have you been?" he asks as he enters the driver's side.

"Obviously not very good," I snap back.

He laughs. "Okay . . . Well, how is your mother?" he says as he puts on his seat belt.

"Let's not go there," I say, and keep my eyes fixed on the dream catcher that dangles from his rearview mirror. Can he be more of a cliché? I know we're Native American, but we used to make fun of all the *pretendians* that hung dream catchers in their cars, and now he has one? Who is this guy? "You dream and drive now?" I say, pointing to it, hoping he remembers how we both laughed at this years ago.

"Did you know that dream catchers are originally from us Ojibwe?"

"No. And I don't care."

"I made this one. I learned to do a lot of things up here," he says, turning to me. "Put on your seat belt, please."

"Fine. Can we go now?" I say as I buckle up.

"Okay. We got lots of time to get to know each other,"

32

he says, and turns the key. The engine wakes up, coughs, then roars to life.

I know it doesn't really make sense, but I'm so mad at him for having this Jeep. When I was a kid, I thought that one day my mom and I'd get him a Jeep like this for his birthday or Christmas. Or maybe he'd get me this Jeep when I turned sixteen. But no, he took a crap on all of that and went and got the Jeep for himself. What a jerk.

We pull onto the main street, which is lined by large towering trees on both sides of the road. The wind whistles loudly through the open top of the Jeep, but still my dad tries to talk over it. "I was afraid I wasn't gonna recognize you, but you look almost exactly as I pictured in my head," he says.

"You look nothing like how I pictured," I say. "You had red puffy cheeks and glassy eyes last time I saw you."

He nods. "I'm a different person now." He keeps his eyes on the road, as if he was saying it more for himself to hear.

"Whatever. So, is there a plan? Am I supposed to chop wood, rake leaves, and discover the true value of life through hard work and blistered fingers?" I ask.

"Why don't we just go with the flow, kiddo," he says.

"Only dead fish go with the flow," I reply. "And don't call me kiddo."

"That's right. You're a big tough guy now. Doing big things, I hear. Your mother told me about all the stuff she found under your bed."

Somehow him mentioning my bed makes me feel like he stumbled into my room. A room he used to tuck me into at night. A room he used to read stories to me in. A room he left. He has no right to enter my room. And definitely no right to judge me for what is under my bed.

"Don't try to parent me. That train sailed a long time ago. I'm only here because of Mom. And stop saying *your mother*. It's weird. It makes it sound like you don't know her. In fact, don't talk about her at all. I don't like it," I say.

"I'll call her your mother because she is your mother. If you don't like how it makes you feel, then maybe you should—"

"Ugh. Just stop. No more talking about her. Just say okay, okay?"

"Fine. Okay . . . And it's 'that ship sailed a long time ago.' Not train. Although you can say 'that train left the station a long time ago,'" he adds.

"I was being ironic. Obviously if that train sailed a long time ago, that means it sank. It's dead. Like this conversation should be," I say.

"Oh, you were being clever? You got that from me. Your mother is the smart one, but I was always the clever—"

"Do you ever stop talking?" I ask.

"Too much too soon. I get it." He lets a breeze of silence pass by us before adding, "You still like music?" and before I can respond, he turns on his radio—and blasts it.

An old R&B love song cracks on, which is the exact

opposite of the vibe in this Jeep right now. But neither of us want to acknowledge that, so neither of us change the station. We both listen to the slow love ballad as we stare straight ahead. If I wasn't so mad right now, I'd probably laugh. Ugh. The singer is talking about crawling like a sexy jaguar across the floor to her lover. This is so wrong . . . And hilarious . . . But I keep my face solid as stone. I will not laugh. I will not.

We drive deeper into the woods, where the sun must not be permitted because as we roll down the road, it gets real dark real fast. The trees are now on my left, my right, behind me, in front of me, and even above me. It's a dark wooden world decorated with leaves and absolutely no sunlight. Our headlights flood on, and I manage to catch the sign as we whip by. It reads GRAND PORTAGE INDIAN RESERVATION. Directly under it reads GICHI-ONIGAMING.

Even though I'm Native American, I don't know much about the culture. We moved away so my dad could work in Duluth, and in a big city, there's a whole slew of cultures to adopt. In my neighborhood, it was mostly white people. So I learned to fit in with white stuff like skateboarding, baseball, and how to be an awful dancer.

The only time I really explored my culture was when we played cowboys and Indians down by Enger Tower with our Super Soaker water cannons. I was always the only Indian taking on the entire US Cavalry. And I was always outnumbered and outgunned, but . . . I quickly made a name for myself. I once took out eleven pale-faced cowboys before I was taken down and soaked from head to toe. They called me the Chippe-Wa-Wa, short for Chippewa water warrior, but as we all got older, we put the water cannons down and picked up other things. Most of the kids picked up sports, some became nerds and picked up books, some became cool and picked up girls . . . but a small handful of us started getting into trouble. We picked up things that weren't ours.

I fell into that crowd because of everything that was happening in my life. I didn't want to be at home, where my mom was stressed out and my dad's chair was empty, so I chose to stick with the kids that stayed out the latest.

"You live in a forest?" I ask.

"Technically right outside of it. We have a house, a ranch, really."

"We? Who's we?" I ask.

He shifts uncomfortably in his bucket seat and avoids looking at me. "Wendy and I."

Wait. Who the heck is Wendy? Does he . . . Did he start a new family? I hate him so much. But this isn't about me right now . . . How could he do this to my mom? "Hold on . . . Does mom know?" I ask more with my teeth than with my lips.

"I don't know how much your mother keeps you in the loop about these things, but yes, she's well aware of Wendy," he says.

"Bullshit. She would have told me," I snap.

"Language!"

"You're not my dad!"

"I am too your dad," he says.

"No. You're not. You were, once. But a lot has changed since then."

"I'm still your father. Like it or not. And under my roof, you'll respect me. No swearing. And absolutely no stealing."

"Oh, so you're the law now? Well, guess what? I happen to be someone who breaks the law. So I'll say what I want and take whatever I want," I say.

He holds up one finger. It immediately throws me back to my childhood. He'd always hold up one finger when people were arguing. It was weird then, and it's weird now. He explained it by saying all it takes to win a fight was one finger. It still doesn't make sense, but somehow it calms me down. I guess it still works. We're no longer arguing.

"Whatever," I say, and roll my eyes away from him.

"Wegodogwen," he replies.

"What?"

"It means 'whatever' in Ojibwe. If you're going to pout, at least learn something while doing it," he says.

"Whatever," I repeat.

I wonder if my mom told him about everything. I hope she didn't tell him how I used to cry every day and night for an entire year after he left. But that doesn't matter now. I don't miss him anymore. I buried him in the backyard of

37

my brain and tried to forget he ever existed. And it's obvious he doesn't miss me or my mom, now that he has a Wendy!

Ugh. I hate her already. She sounds like a fast food hamburger. And why is my mom talking to him, anyway? She should move on, like I did.

Do they talk about how disappointing a son I am?

"You break the rules, I send you back. And your mother will definitely tell that handsome judge about it. And you know what he'll do, right? Final chance, I think he called it?"

My mom even told him about Judge Mason? "He's not handsome. He's average-looking," I say.

"That's not what I heard. I also heard he keeps his word, so follow the rules."

"You want to play dad for a little while, fine. But I'm not calling this Wendy lady Mom. I already don't like her."

"And why's that?" he asks, his eyes still on the road.

"Because she likes you."

"You're still angry with me, Benny. But hopefully your time here will change that."

"I seriously doubt it."

"Well, doubting is halfway to believing, so I'll take it," he says, and turns left, off the road.

We drive into an open field. Light rushes back to us and lights up everything around me. It's almost as if the sun missed us and is now greeting us with a huge warm hug. The road we're on now is made of mud, and he steps on the gas a little to kick it up. I see a side-eye smirk from him, and there's a part of me that wants to shout, "Faster!" but I don't want him to think there's any chance for us bonding—because there isn't. Not at all. I swear.

We drive up a hill, tires sliding side to side, mud flying everywhere as we come to a large red-painted ranch. OMG, my dad lives on a farm. There are ducks, goats, and a flipping pig milling about. Is my dad a farmer? I hope he doesn't expect me to milk a cow or a goat or a pig. Do people milk pigs? Well, even if they do, I don't. I'm not milking anything. I need to come up with a few rules of my own. "I'm not a farmer, and I have no intentions of becoming one, ever," I say.

"Good to know. Random, but good to know," he replies.

"Not very random. We did just pull up to a farm," I say, waving a hand in the direction of the goats.

"Relax. They're pets. Well, not pets, more like family, really," he says. "It's my rescue ranch."

"You rescue animals now?" I ask. "Who are you?"

"You'll see, animals are just like us, once you take the time to get to know them."

"You may be a pig, Wendy may be a cow, but I am not like some stupid farm animal."

He smiles. "Of horse you're not," he says, and laughs at his own joke.

But I don't laugh. It wasn't that funny. "Your mother would have laughed at that one," he adds.

"Oh, yes, let's talk about her again since it went so well the last time," I say.

"Okay . . . So, your mom, has she been dating anyone?" he asks.

Did he really just ask me that? "I was being sarcastic," I say.

"You were being fantastic?"

"Sarcastic!"

"Snaptastic?"

"That's not even a word, and also shut up," I say.

He laughs. I almost feel a haha rising in my throat, so I focus on the farm. Ugh. Even these smelly animals almost make me want to smile. The goats are kind of cute.

I need to remember why I hate him. *Think. He left. Mama crying. Drunk. Wendy. Growing up with no dad. Shouting. Crying. Wendy. This stupid Beep Beep Jeep.*

Grand Portage. There's nothing grand about it. It sucks. And everyone in it sucks, especially him. And Wendy.

My anger rushes back. I'm too pissed to say anything. I want this Jeep to tip over, and I want him to drown in the muddy mess that he made of my life.

"Well, if she's not, it's understandable. She has a lot on her plate," he says.

I'm not sure if he means that I've been too much of a heavy load in my mom's life for her to have one of her own, or if he wants to twist the knife into my ribs by admitting she has a lot on her plate because she had to do everything on her own while he was out dating girls named Wendy and living with goats. Either way, he's a jerk for saying it.

I just want to stare at the ducks now. So I do. I stare at the stupid ducks near a muddy pond. Lucky ducks. They can fly away whenever they want.

CHAPTER 5

ANIMOSH-NOODIN (DOG WIND)

We pull up to the house. It's not very big, which is strange, because it's surrounded by so much land. I guess they want to make room for more animals. Elephants, maybe? Giraffes? Lions? Tigers? Bears? Ugh . . . I'm here all because of that bear. If I had just walked away, none of this would be happening. I'd be home, with all my stuff. Making money.

The Jeep stops, and I immediately jump out so I can get further away from this guy that used to be my dad. One step in, and my feet sink deep into the mud, swallowing my shoes. Why can't he live in the city like a normal person? I grab my backpack and suitcase; the weight of it makes me stumble backward. I try to grab the Jeep, but I'm falling. I lose my balance, and my butt lands in the mud. Splash. My dad laughs.

I try to get up. My hand sinks into the thick, slushy brown dirt, kind of locking me in place.

"That's a good look on you," he says, and makes his way around the Jeep, stopping in front of me.

"You could have warned me," I say.

"Warned you of what? That mud could be . . . muddy?" he replies, and laughs again—this time offering me his hand.

I take it, not with my clean hand, but with the one covered in mud. He accepts it anyway and launches me out of my mud seat. I stand, covered in brown from the waist down. And now that I have a better look, I see he pulled up and lined the passenger door directly above the mud puddle. He did this on purpose. I'm 96 percent sure of it.

"Looks like we may have to hose you down," he says, while wiping his muddy hand on his jeans.

"You're not hosing me down," I say, even though a part of me did imagine boot camp consisting of getting hosed down and stripped of all your confidence like they do in military movies. They have to break you down to build you up. That's how they brainwash you.

But this isn't the boot camp, right? My dad wouldn't run it. The only running he's capable of is running away. And running his mouth. And running up his tab at the bar. But being in charge of a boot camp? No way.

"Windy Wendy ain't gonna let you waltz into the house covered in earth poop."

"Windy Wendy?"

"That's what I call her. But only sometimes, when she can't hear me," he says.

"Why?"

"She's a gust of a gal. You'll see," he says.

"Okay. That makes no sense, but okay."

As I fling the mud off my right hand, two dogs come galloping from around the house to meet us. They are large like wolves. My dad is tackled by them as soon as he kneels down to welcome them. He proceeds to roll around on the ground with them, covering himself in earth poop. I guess he's getting the hose too. "Gimoodishkiiwinini," my dad shouts from the ground and points at me.

"What does that mean?" I ask.

"Thief," he says.

As soon as his words leave his lips, both dogs stop and turn their gaze to me. One is black. One is brown. Both are coated in mud. And both are growling.

"I wouldn't move if I were you," he says.

I freeze. I never had a dog. The only pet I had was a rat named Animosh, which means dog in Ojibwe. Rats are dogs for people who live in small apartments.

"What do I do?" I whisper.

"Slowly . . . run," he replies in a loud whisper.

"I thought you said don't move," I snap back.

"Too late for that. They smell your goshi."

"What's a goshi?"

"They smell your fear. You need to run. Slowly."

"How does someone run slowly?" I ask, feeling my heart beat faster as my eyes fix on their sharp white teeth as they continue to territorially growl.

"Like in slow motion?" he says. It sounds like a question.

"That's ridiculous," I say.

"Ridiculous, you say?" My dad narrows his eyes and smiles. "Sic him!" he shouts.

Both dogs launch themselves toward me. I immediately try to run, but my legs can't keep up with my frightened rabbit feet. So I slip into the mud and my body splashes onto the thick and frothy ground—face-first.

The dogs charge through the mud, and I close my eyes, bracing for impact. I hope for whatever happens to be quick and painless. I imagine muddy blood and bloody mud everywhere. A crime scene that requires heavy boots and a steel stomach.

I was sent here to die. My parents conspired together to get rid of me. These dogs will eat me alive, even my bones, leaving no trace of me. I can hear it now. *He got on the bus in Duluth, but never arrived in Grand Portage.* It will be an unsolved mystery forever.

The two hounds draw nearer; I take a deep breath as their bodies collide into mine like two trains hitting a wall at once. Here it is. Death. Here come the teeth. The inevitable bite down. The dismemberment. But all I feel is . . . What is that? It's slimy and wet . . . Are those tongues? Is one in my ear?

I open my eyes and find myself completely pinned to the ground, with both dogs licking, slobbering, and drooling all over my face. All of this happening while a loud, belly-filled laugh rolls through the air.

I pick my head up and see my dad beside himself, laughing hysterically, holding his gut, like if he were to let go, his intestines would be spilling onto his muddy boots.

I wrestle up, fending off the two canines as they do everything in their power to drench me. After a few failed attempts, I finally make it to my feet.

"I almost crapped my pants," I shout at him, who has just now finally stopped laughing.

"Did you think I said 'sic him'? I said 'soak him,'" he manages to say, erupting in a second wave of laughter.

His face streams with tears, and his hair bounces with each chuckle. It almost sends a spark of anger through my body, seeing him so happy at my expense. I remind myself that he doesn't deserve happiness. After all, he robbed me of mine.

His cheeks used to be puffy and red. Now they are sharp, and sunken in. They even cast small shadows under the bone. Being happy looks really good on him, but I doubt it will last. If he's good at anything, it is letting people down. He taps his thigh, and both dogs rush back to him and sit at his feet, awaiting his next command.

"You didn't run slow enough," he says.

"That doesn't make sense. And now I smell like dog. No.

Now I smell like two dogs," I say, wiping my wet hands onto my muddy jeans, which does nothing but add more mud to my everywhere.

"Well, introduce yourself."

"You want me to introduce myself to your dogs?"

"They're your roommates for the next however long we got, so yeah, you should introduce yourself, obviously," he says, like it's strange I even asked.

"Hi, dogs. I'm Benny. What are your names, Muddy and Muddier?"

"They're dogs, kiddo. They don't speak English," my dad says in a tone suggesting I'm the strange one here.

"I know that, but you said . . . Never mind," I say.

"This is Rolex." He points to the brown dog.

"And this is Casio." He points to the black dog.

"That's their real names?" I ask.

"Of course. They're my watch dogs," he says.

"Hi, Rolex and Casio," I say.

"We have a third dog, Apple, but she's out on a hike with Wendy."

"Let me guess, she's white?" I say.

"Wendy or the dog?" he asks.

"Your dog. Not Wendy."

"Both are white. Apple and Wendy."

He snaps his fingers, and Casio and Rolex go running off into the enormous field. It takes a second for me to process his words. Wendy is white. He has a white girlfriend. I

47

don't care about her skin color, not really. I mean, there are plenty of good white people in the world, but I do care that he has a girlfriend that isn't a Native American woman that I call Mom. And the way he just tosses it out there makes me mad all over again.

Before I can even get madder, my thoughts are washed away by a strong stream of water hitting me in the thighs. I look up at my dad, and he is firing his hose at me, at full strength, laughing while aiming. Soaking. Drenching. Engulfing me. While intermittently turning the hose on himself, dousing his entire body. I can't help but laugh as the spray hits his face, sending him back stumbling, tripping over the coiled hose's neck and falling back into the mud like he's one of those funny comedians in those movies we used to watch when I was little. It's a clown fighting a water snake. We'd laugh, rewind it, watch it again. Laugh again. He loved Buster Keaton and Charlie Chaplin. Which made me love them. Now I avoid them.

But . . . at least the water is warm. Or maybe it's not—maybe it just seems warm compared to the blistering cold air. I wonder if I'll freeze and turn to ice if I stay out here long enough? I don't want to find out. My fingers hurt.

"It's called Dog Wind," he says to me as he rises to his feet.

"What is?"

"The wind here. She starts barking, letting you know she's here. Then, she licks your face, getting a feel for you,

48

letting you get a feel for her . . . but if you stay out here any longer without a scarf, coat, and mittens, then that dog starts biting. And she's got a nasty bite."

"Down, girl!" I shout to the wind, grab my stuff, and run toward the front door.

"No shoes in the house!" he shouts as I reach the screen door.

He's right. A pile of muddy shoes pyramids the front porch. My dad has very big feet. Wendy has small feet. I kick off my shoes, peel back the screen, open the front door, and step inside.

CHAPTER 6

AGASSI-AKI (IT'S A SMALL WORLD)

My dad tosses me a towel and points down the hallway. I guess it's shower time. I open my suitcase and pull out an outfit; a new red long-sleeve hooded sweatshirt I stole last week from the mall and a pair of designer jeans that still have the tags on them. Good thing my mom didn't rifle through my clothes too thoroughly, or I'd be wearing old threads for my new adventure here.

I take a look around the house, and I am immediately confused. It's full of places . . . Sections of the house are broken up into various places on earth. It looks like a travel agent broke in and left their career here before they took the TV and split.

I'm currently standing in what appears to be the Hawaiian section, where the walls are painted orange and blue to resemble the island sky, with palm trees plastered over the paint. Coconuts litter the floor, which actually has small mounds of sand on the carpet. The wooden tiki shelves have those little Hawaiian hula dancers on each end. There's a ukulele and a miniature surfboard propped up against the wall. And a large stuffed turtle lies at my feet.

And just a few steps over, the next section of the house is dedicated to Los Angeles. On that wall is painted the summer blue sky with puffy white clouds hanging over the iconic Hollywood sign. On the LA shelves are rows of books about movies, actors, and rock and roll bands. A camera is propped up on a tripod, and small movie posters and postcards are tacked on the walls, clouding parts of the California skyline. The floor even has three hand-drawn Hollywood stars plastered to it. They are made out of cardboard and duct taped onto the carpet. The names are written in gold glitter. One says *Wendy*. One says *Tommy*, which is my dad's name, and the last one says *George*.

Who is George?

Behind me, on the adjacent wall, is a shrine to Tibet. Beautiful colorful photographs line the walls. A jolly, fat golden Buddha sits on the center of the shelf. Ceramic elephants, cows, and monkeys sit on its lower tiers. Thick red beads hang down, nearly touching the potted plants on the ground. And a string of multicolored Tibetan prayer flags is draped from one section to the other . . . but stops before the next section begins, which is Australia: crocodiles, kangaroos, a framed photo of the Hemsworth brothers, and a ceramic koala bear.

It's like that one Disneyland ride; it's a small world after all.

"I guess you're wondering why we got our house set up like the aki?" my dad says.

"What's aki mean?"

"Earth. Have you forgotten all Ojibwe?"

"I've been busy. And no, I'm not wondering why the house is like this, because I don't care."

I step away from the Australia installation. But a thought hits me, stinging like a sad bee trapped somewhere inside of me, attacking my ribs.

"Who's George? Wait. You know what, I don't care about that either," I say, and walk toward the hall faster than my words can travel to my dad—so he doesn't have time to respond.

I walk past the great white shark painted on the end of the Aussie wall and give a quick look at Japan's decorations on the far side, before I enter the hallway and search for the shower.

There are three doors in front of me. Three rooms. I'm guessing the farthest one back is my dad's room, which also means Wendy's room. The thought revives the anger in me. What a home wrecker. He stumbles out of our apartment and ends up in this huge multicountried house. A house! I've never lived in a house, and this Wendy-haver gets one?

And now he's sober? Where was my sober dad? Wendy gets to have the funny, good-looking version. This is not fair. He sucks. She sucks too. George sucks too, whoever he is . . . They can all skip these countries and go straight to my butt and kiss it.

I open the first door and loud gunshots fill my ears. It sends me back a step. For a split second, I look for a corner to hide behind, but the walls around me aren't shot up and full of holes, so I open the door wider. The only light comes from the far side of the room. A large screen is mounted on the wall. And now all the gunfire makes sense. It's a first-person-shooter video game.

The screen is taken up largely by a machine gun mowing down a dozen or so zombies. But who's playing? I step in to see. Through the flashes of light in the mostly dark room, I see the silhouette of a kid lying in bed, with his headset on, staring fixedly at the screen.

"Hello?" I say, but he doesn't hear me. He just keeps killing zombies.

He hasn't noticed me because he's wearing one of those fancy headsets. I stole a few of those before and sold each one for thirty bucks back in Duluth. He is speaking in loud whispers, just not to me. In between shots, he's saying something into his headset. I stay still and listen. He repeats, "On your left," "Nice shot," and the occasional, "Cover me, I need to reload." Now I get it. He's playing with a bunch of gamers online. What a nerd.

I step back out of his room and slowly close the door before he mistakes me for a real zombie. I ain't looking to get shot today. Game or no game, I don't like guns pointed at me. I release his doorknob and go toward the next door. Then it clicks . . . That was George. What is a George doing here? Why does he have a room in my dad's house?

Three steps later, anger erupts inside my gut like a sleeping volcano waking up. I've been replaced by a George! And worse, a nerdy gamer! My dad not only walked out on his wife and found a Wendy, but he walked out on his son and found a George. I hate him. I hate Wendy. I hate Grand Portage. But . . . I still really need to shower, so I'll explore this hatred after I rinse all this mud off me. It has just occurred to me that on a ranch full of animals, some of this earth poop may very well be animal poop too.

I open the door and step into the bathroom. I try to calm my nerves by starting the water immediately. Hot water soothes, I tell myself. My dad is a deadbeat, but hot water soothes. Wendy is a home wrecker, but hot water soothes. George is my replacement, but hot water soothes. I test this theory as I strip naked and step into the shower. I'm so mad I could scream. But I don't, because hot water soothes.

I scrub myself down and try my best to rinse away all my thoughts of my dad, my mom, Judge Mason, Wendy, George, those two mud hounds, and this in-the-middle-of-nowhere place called Grand Portage. It's difficult to do, but the steam does its job. The madness subsides as I stand

54

under the showerhead and soak in the heat. All the mad and all the mud fall off my body and travel down the drain.

I put on my clean clothes and exit the bathroom. George's door is still shut. There must be quite the zombie epidemic in that room. I hope he runs out of ammo and gets eaten alive—slowly.

I walk down the hall, realizing I don't yet know where I'll be sleeping. Where's my room? There are only two bedrooms in this house. So I return to the only place I know, the global living room.

Maybe it's because I'm only one minute out of the shower, but I can't help but feel that there's a warmness to this place, or should I say to these places. Maybe that's just how living in a house feels. It's like the three little pigs story. When you're homeless, it feels like wherever you sleep is made of straw. A slight breeze can cause your whole life to crash down around you. When you live in an apartment, it's like your home is made of sticks. It's not great, but it's better than straw. It won't keep you warm, but you aren't going to freeze to death either. But living in a house like this, well, no huffing and puffing from any wolf is going to knock this place down. It's like a giant brick oven. No drafts, no chills, just toasty air that hugs you as you enter each room. I wish my mom could feel this warmth. She always sleeps in doubled-up sweaters.

Life is unfair. The disappointing dad gets the big house, and the hardworking mom gets the tiny apartment with a family living above us, below us, to our left and to our right. And when one family plays music, we all gotta listen to that music. When one family vacuums, we might as well all vacuum, and sadly, when one family has a screaming match, then we all have to hear it.

My eyes sweep across the room, but no one's here. Oh, I didn't even notice that Jamaica was in that corner, and Scotland is in the other. But I don't want to explore them yet; I'm too hungry to travel. I'd love to be able to stand in the Italy part of the room and have someone bring me a super cheesy pizza. That would be awesome.

I walk back down the hall to see if my dad is in his room. Even though I don't like him, I know better than to enter another man's kitchen and start eating his food.

I tap gently on his door, then knock harder, both getting no response. I check the handle. It's unlocked. I open the door and step inside. The room is less of a bedroom and more of a workshop. And not just any workshop, but an animal workshop.

There are dozens of figurines on every shelf, every counter. Not the cheap kind you see at gas stations and gift shops near the register, but very detailed sculpture-like animals made from clay and painted to a flawless accuracy that almost makes me think the animal posed for hours for whoever was making it. There are caribou, deer, wolves, loons, eagles, turtles, and even a moose . . . And that's just the shelf

I can see. There are two or three shelves behind it, all filled with more animals. This room is a freaking zoo.

And at the large oak desk in the corner is my dad. Painting the eye of a ceramic squirrel. Did my dad make all of these? Is he an artist now? What the hell? Why didn't he make animals when I knew him? His interests back then were whiskey and crying at all hours of the night. My stomach growls, reminding me why I'm in here.

"You really like animals, don't you?" I say, and his hand stops.

He swivels around in his chair to face me. He's wearing silly glasses that make his eyes five times larger. He takes them off and folds them, placing them on the desk.

"This is an ajidamoo. A squirrel. And these are my Awesiinh," he says, and points to his collection.

"Awesiinh? What's that mean?" I ask.

"That's the name of the collection. It means 'wild animal,'" he says.

"You still speak Ojibwe, huh? I quit after you left" I say, having forgotten nearly everything he taught me when I was younger, and only hearing it nowadays under my mom's breath when she's angry. She begged me to keep studying it, saying how important it is to know our mother tongue, but I found better ways to steal my time: by stealing. Plus, Ojibwe always reminded me of him, and all I wanted to do was forget him, so I forgot Ojibwe as much as I could.

"Many things about me have changed, but not everything," he says.

"Well, you still did what you did," I say. "You can pretend all you want to be a 'changed man,' but I know who you are."

"I can't change the past, but it doesn't have to be my future," he says. "Or our present."

"Whatever. You sound like a bumper sticker."

He laughs, and from my stomach, a growl shakes my ribs so loudly that my dad shoots his eyes to my belly.

"You're that bakade?" he asks.

"If that means hungry, yeah, I'm starving."

"Me too. Why don't you make us some lunch," he says.

"I'm not much of a cook," I say.

"That was the old Benny. Maybe the new Benny would like to give it a shot. After all, we are in Cook County."

"Fine. I'll 'give it a shot,' but I can't promise what I make will be edible."

He smiles, gets up, and walks out of the room. I look at the one-eyed squirrel, and for a split second, I think about knocking it off his desk, just to watch it shatter—the way he shattered our family and now has the nerve to be an artist. While my mom is barely making rent, he's over here in his big farmhouse painting little animals, making dream catchers and building weird travel spots in his living room. And now he wants me to cook him food. No way!

Before I leave the room, I notice that I am already at

his desk with the squirrel in my hand. All I have to do now is drop it. All I have to do is release my grip, and this squirrel dies.

"I know you want to, but it won't make you feel better. I've been where you are now. And I dropped it," my dad says from behind me.

"Was I the squirrel you dropped?" I ask.

"No. I was the squirrel I dropped. Don't make the same mistake I did. You'll feel worse. Trust me."

"That's the thing . . ." I look him straight in the eye and drop the squirrel. "I don't trust you."

There's no blood or guts or squirrel screams. Just ceramic chunks scattered at my feet.

I walk past him and out of the room. His eyes are filled with a look I have seen in my mother many times: disappointment. I don't care. He's disappointed me my whole life.

But by the time I am halfway through the hall, I realize he is right. I don't feel better. In fact, I feel worse because that squirrel had nothing to do with my dad leaving us. It should have been him who I held up and dropped. He should be in chunks on the floor. He should be in pain, not me. And definitely not the squirrel.

I enter the kitchen and try to act like nothing happened. I don't want to feel bad for killing a ceramic squirrel, and I don't want to get a lecture on how I made the wrong decision by Mr. Wrong Decision himself. I just want something to eat.

He follows me a few seconds later. We must be more

alike than I thought, because he too is acting like the squirrel murder never happened. He is smiling again.

"Everything you need is in here. Hurry up, I'm as hungry as a hippo," he says, and walks out of the kitchen.

Hungry as a hippo. I wonder if his words were intentional. We used to play that game when I was little. Hungry Hungry Hippos. It was our thing. We played it before dinner to work up our appetites, and when my mom would bring in our meals, we'd both pretend to be hippos and scarf down the food as quickly as possible. My mom would watch in horror as we both made a mess and filled our faces with food. Does he play that game with George now?

Little does he know, the only thing I can make that's half decent is a grilled cheese sandwich. So that's exactly what's on the menu for lunch. I know I said I wouldn't cook for him, but I'm way too tired and way too hungry to fight. I'll just make the freaking sandwiches and argue with him when my belly's full. I guess I'm going to smell like cheese again.

Seven minutes later, I carry our plates out of the kitchen. The thought of melted cheese quickens my pace. The sooner I give him his, the sooner I can eat mine.

He's sitting in a beach chair in the Hawaiian section of the living room. He's removed his shirt and is leaning back as if he is sunbathing. He's even drinking a pop through a straw and wearing sunglasses. On the ceiling is a large yellow sun made of construction paper.

"Pull up a chair, it's nice out," he says, and points to a folded beach chair.

I walk up to him and hand him his plate. There's a slight itch inside of me that wants to indulge in this little Hawaiian fantasy. A fake sun is still a sun, right? But I don't. We are not friends. It will be better for everyone if he gets that through his thick head.

"They're a little burnt," I say.

"That's okay. I have sunscreen," he says, and pulls out an invisible sunblock tube and squeezes it onto his hands. He mushes his hands together and smears the invisible sunblock onto his grilled cheese sandwich.

"Really?" I ask.

"Either sit and eat or find a flight off the island," he says.

"What?"

"You're blocking my sun, son," he says, and brushes his hand into the air, signaling that my shadow is interfering with his imaginary sun rays.

I don't want him calling me son. Not ever again. But I don't tell him this because my mouth is full of grilled cheese. I'll tell him later.

I step aside, and he smiles. "After we eat, I was thinking we can visit Manido Gizhigans," he says.

"Who's that?" I ask.

He laughs. "Little Spirit Cedar Tree. A four-hundred-year-old cedar growing from the rocks. Tourists aren't allowed to go up to it, but us Ojibwe are. I was thinking we can leave some asemaa under the tree together."

"Is that what people do around here? Go see old trees? There are millions of trees around us, and you want to go see another one? That's fun to you? This isn't Grand Portage. This is Bland Boretage."

"Fine. Maybe another time. When you're ready. I guess you'll just get straight to work, then," he says as he bites into the cheesy sandwich.

"Work? What work?" I ask with my mouth full.

"You didn't think this was a vacation, did you? Boot camp is what I think your mom called it," he says.

Before I can respond, I hear the front door unlock and the shuffling of giant dogs (maybe large rats, maybe wolves) right outside the house. My dad leaps up from his beach chair. His eyes light up with a happiness I haven't seen since I was six. He looks like a little boy on Christmas Eve that just caught a glimpse of Santa.

"Did you make Windy Wendy a grilled cheese?" he whispers to me.

"Uh, no. Obviously."

"But she's always hungry," he says.

"Not my problem," I say.

"Oh, but it is. There's nothing scarier than a hungry Wendy. We must always make one for Wendy. Here, you give me this piece, and I'll give her one of mine," he says as he snatches half of my grilled cheese and puts it on his plate, having it appear that there is now a whole grilled cheese sandwich waiting for her to gobble up.

The door opens. My dad throws on his shirt and takes a few steps, leaving Hawaii.

Rolex, Casio, and Apple (the white dog) rush past me and dart straight for the kitchen, leaving us humans alone in the living room. Wendy enters, wearing a blue jogger's track-suit. She is pale white and has long red hair. I immediately think of the American flag. Red, white, and blue. There are even fifty stars too, but they're not coming from her; they are in my dad's eyes when he looks at her. He's so giddy. It makes me want to vomit.

He hands the plate to Wendy as she approaches us, which causes her to smile. Her teeth are so white, and as she gets closer, I see her face. She's beautiful and plain at the same time. I want to search her face for things I can hate and mentally make fun of, but the truth is, she is as pretty as those Viking actresses on TV. She looks tough enough to hold her own in a dark alley but still sweet enough to give up a grilled cheese sandwich for. Ugh. I really don't like her. My mom is way prettier. And probably way smarter too.

Wendy finally looks at me, and her eyes are as blue as the Hawaiian sky painted on the walls behind us. If she stood perfectly still, she'd look like one of the animals my dad makes but hasn't painted yet. She is porcelain white. Probably the whitest person I have ever seen.

"Her eyes. Don't stare too long, or you'll begin to float away," my dad says.

"What are you talking about?" I say, looking away from Wendy as she bites into her sandwich.

"I call them skeyes. When I first saw her, I floated fifty feet up, they had to toss me a rope to bring me back down," he says to me.

"That never happened," Wendy says in between bites. "I'm the proud owner of two boring blues. Hi, I'm Wendy." She offers me her hand.

I don't take her hand. I don't want this Wendy lady to think we're on good terms. We're not. She stole my dad. That makes her my enemy. My porcelain-pale, boring-blue-eyed enemy.

My dad notices my snub and tries to calm the seas between us by plopping the last bite of his sandwich onto her plate. "She'll eat the entire house if you let her," he says.

Wendy laughs and finally puts her hand back down to her waist. "Thank you for the sandwich," she says to me, while chewing her final bite. "I know your father didn't make this. It's good to see we have another cook in the house. I was getting lonely."

"Well, this is Cook County," my dad adds.

"You already used that joke. It wasn't funny the first time either," I say.

Wendy laughs. "Well, still, thank you for feeding me," she says.

"That's all I can make, really. Grilled cheeses and some-times scrambled eggs. Half the time they come out wrong."

"Only half the time? I'll take those odds any day. Like tomorrow," she says.

Did she just imply I'm making her breakfast tomorrow morning? My dad is right. She's always hungry. I mean, who plans out breakfast while finishing lunch? And is this part of boot camp? Was I sent here to make breakfast for the people who ruined my life? How is that going to rehabilitate me?

"We have any chips? Chips are so good with a sandwich," she says.

My dad takes her plate and and heads into the kitchen. "I'll check."

Wendy and I are alone. I stare at her. She stares at me. I will not float away.

"So, Benny . . . What's your specialty?" she asks.

"I just told you. All I can make are grilled—"

"No, I mean, your specialty. Is it pickpocketing, shoplifting, grand theft auto, burglary?"

I smile, even though I should probably be insulted. "I guess you can say shoplifting. Although I'm not a bad pickpocket, if I'm being honest."

"Well, hopefully you'll discover new skills, ones less damaging to your soul while you're here. My one rule is you do not steal while you live under this roof," she says, and places her hands on her hips, the same way in those Western movies when the actor tells everyone that there's a new sheriff in town.

"Relax, I'm not going to steal from you," I assure her, which is most likely a lie since I have stolen from my own mom, a few bucks here and there. And that I already regret, but I'd have no issue stealing from my mom's replacement.

"Whoever you steal from, it always ends with you stealing from me," she says.

Another bumper sticker speaker. "How is me stealing from someone else also stealing from you?" I ask.

"You steal away trust. And I, for one, hate nothing more than not being able to trust someone. There're miles and miles of forest out there. It wouldn't be hard to hide a scrawny body like yours if something of mine goes missing . . . Don't screw this up, Benny," she says as she walks past me, presumably to help my dad hunt down those elusive chips.

Wendy is so strange. One minute she's super nice, and the next minute she's threatening to hide my dead body in a forest. I can see why my dad likes her. She's unpredictable. And unpredictable is never boring. Even if her blue eyes are.

"Wendy," I say before she reaches Australia.

She turns around and raises her eyebrows. "Where will I be staying?" I ask.

"In the garage, with the watch dogs and all the important stuff. Remember my rule, kid," she says and points to a door. "Don't worry. It's insulated. Technically it's the largest room in the house, you lucky duck."

I have to stay in a garage? With three smelly dogs? I open the door and step inside. It's a large room with an entire back catalogue of animals lining the shelves. This must be dad's storage. Half of them are not yet painted, and the other half have SOLD stickers stuck to them. I should smash them all and cause real trouble for him, but I'm here to be a better person, right? I owe it to my mom to at least try out this boot camp thing. I wonder when it is going to begin?

Near the window is my bed. A cool-looking mama moose and her two babies are stitched onto the red blanket. The thought of three meese—mooses—moose? sleeping on me every night warms my body. Against another wall are three large dog beds. I hope those giant dogs don't snore. I sit down on the bed and consider taking a nap, wishing this was all just a bad dream. If I fall asleep in my dream, maybe I'll wake up in real life . . . But, ten minutes later, Wendy walks in and tosses me the keys to the Jeep.

"Time for work. You drive," she says.

"I'm thirteen," I say. "I can't drive yet."

She pauses and stares at the keys in my hand. What is she doing? It looks like she's having a conversation in her head. Even her lips are slightly moving.

"You okay?" I ask, which snaps her out of it.

"Your dad can drop us off," she says.

"You don't know how to drive? But you're old," I say.

"I know how to drive. I just don't," she says.

"Back in Duluth, that's just called being lazy," I say.

Her gaze bites my face, "I am not lazy, kid. I just . . ."

"What is it, then? Pretty little white lady needs her big Indian man to drive her around, so she doesn't break a nail?" I ask.

She shows her teeth. "I know what you're doing. You want to rattle me. You want us to seethe at the sight of one another, but it's not going to work. I'm not going to dislike you, Benny. Now matter how hard you try," she says.

"Well, I already don't like you, and if you're too scared to drive, that's fine. I'll just stay here and take a nap," I say.

She takes a deep breath. Half anger, half determination. I know I agitate people. I like getting a rise from them and seeing them squirm in frustration. Anyway, I'm not here to make friends. Especially with someone who replaced my mom. Wendy can go kick rocks . . . But . . . Why isn't she leaving?

"Fine. I'll drive. But you owe me," she says, and walks out of the garage.

I owe her? What the heck is going on?

I follow her out of the house, and I'm immediately met with the crisp cold air that reminds me that this is no dream. I'm no longer in Duluth. I'm really here. Ugh.

The chill somehow sneaks past my sweatshirt, past my skin, and finds a way to attack my bones. After a few agonizing steps, I give up on walking and run to the Jeep. This time, I avoid the mud puddle and shimmy my body alongside the Jeep to the passenger door. Wendy, however, wears no more than her long-sleeve sweatshirt and sweatpants, and walks like she's taking a stroll through a butterfly garden in spring. And what is that around her neck? The golden scarf I stole. Did she go through my stuff? What happened to trust? She climbs into the Jeep and slides the key into the ignition. "I can do this," she says.

"Yeah, obviously," I say.

"You're right, obviously. Oh, and thanks for the scarf. That was really sweet of you," she says as she roars the engine awake from its sleep. "Your father said you got it for me. How did you know I love gold?"

"Look at history. White people love gold. Just remember this sweet gesture before you plan on dragging me through the woods wondering where to bury me," I say.

She laughs. Yep. And there it is. No wonder my dad leaps to his feet whenever she asks him to do something for her. It's to keep her happy, and if she's happy, she'll be smiling. And to see that smile is worth doing whatever chore there is. I really need to remember that I dislike her. Wendy is bad. Wendy is really pretty, but very bad. She wrecks homes. She steals dads. I mean, I steal things too, but not dads away from moms and sons. She's a next-level thief.

"Don't look at me like that," she says.

"Like what?" I ask.

"Like you're developing a crush on me," she says. "I know how boys are. Eyes forward."

"Seriously," I say, and point my fluttered eyes forward

like she asked. "I was actually thinking of how much I dislike you . . . Plus, you're too old for me," I add.

"Aww, a woman can never get tired of hearing that," she says, and laughs. "Say it again."

"Which part? How much I dislike you or you being too old?" I ask.

"The old one."

"You're *way* too old for me," I say.

"Music to my way too old ears. But still, eyes forward," she reminds me.

We're halfway out of the dirt trail near the main road before I wonder where we're going. Her eyes are so focused on the road and her arms are stiff, gripping the steering wheel so tight it is turning her pink knuckles white. It's like she's never driven before. But I'm not going to say anything about it, because I'm in here, and the last thing I want is to have her have a meltdown while driving . . . But every car is passing us. She's driving so slowly. What's her deal?

"Where is this boot camp anyway?" I ask.

"Oh, you're going to help me at my shop first," she says, without looking at me. "Boot camp comes later."

"You own a shop?"

"It's small and not very fancy, but it's all mine," she says.

"What kind of store is it?" I ask.

She turns to me and gives me a most sinister grin. "A place where magic lives."

"Magic isn't real," I say.

"Sure it is. In my shop, you can be anyone, do anything, go anywhere," she adds.

"Are you a travel agent or something?" I ask, which would explain all the countries in her house. She should have listened to the old saying that you should never bring your work home with you.

She laughs. "No. I own a bookstore."

Boring. Boring. Boring. I hate bookstores. I hate libraries. They are the most boring places humankind has ever created. Even a thief like me couldn't find something worth stealing in a bookstore.

"I'm not much of a book person. Maybe I can help out in some other way?" I ask.

"Sure. You can always help Tommy with his plumbing gig. That is, if you don't mind digging deep into dirty toilets all day?" she says. "Should we turn around?"

"He's an animal maker, an animal rescuer, and a plumber?" I ask.

"Yep. That man can do it all. Creates the creatures on Monday, saves them on Tuesday, and scoops the poop on Wednesday. Should I turn around, or what?"

"No. Not many things are worse than being surrounded by books all day, but sticking my hands into a bowl full of someone's exits is definitely one of them," I say. "Bookstore it is."

"That's the spirit," she says. "Exits, huh? I never heard of crap being called exits before . . . I guess it makes sense."

71

"I never heard of mud being called earth poop before. I guess we learn something new every day," I say.

"That's probably the smartest thing you have ever said," she says.

"You just met me."

"I know, but I can just tell you're not the brightest firefly in the field. But don't worry. You're young. You still have a lot of glowing up to do."

I bet she thought that was clever. She and my dad probably sit around all day and compete for who's most clever in the house. But to me, they're both dorks. Being clever is a waste of time. She reaches over and turns on the radio. The music plays. It's a rap song from the Minnesota rapper Kristoff Krane. He's huge in Duluth. This makes it even harder to dislike her. She's cool. She likes rap. I wish she liked country or something that I could complain about.

"Oh, I love this song," she says as she raps along.

I watch her in awe. She even knows the words. If I didn't dislike her so much, I'd probably even sing along with her right now. I know all the words too. But I won't chime in. She's the enemy.

"Eyes forward, Benjamin!"

CHAPTER 7

THE MAZINA'IGAN-MAKAK [BOOK BOX]

We pull into a small parking lot, right off Highway 61. The sign hanging above the door says THE BOOK BOX and looks like a book cover. I bet she thinks that was a clever idea too. I wonder if my dad, the now artist-plumber, made it. I scan the surrounding area. On one side of the store is an old-looking church, and on the other side is a huge casino. I guess a quaint little bookstore is the perfect way to separate the saints from the sinners.

We park the Jeep and step outside. Somehow, it's even colder now. I need to get a jacket soon. I stuff my hands into my pockets and follow Wendy to the door. She unlocks it and flips the CLOSE YOUR EYES sign over. The sign now reads OPEN YOU MIND. That's cute, but . . .

"Shouldn't it say 'open YOUR mind,' not 'YOU mind'?" I ask.

"Yes. That's just to make sure whoever enters this place can read. Readers are a must for a bookstore. You just passed the first test. You may enter," she says with a smile.

So, before boot camp, I'm stuck here in book camp. This sucks.

"It warms my heart every time a young reader approaches me and points it out. And it's always kids, never adults. Strange, huh?"

"The adults probably assume you can't spell," I say.

"Adults always like to assume, don't they?"

"You just did."

I follow her inside. The shop is filled with my dad's ceramic animals. And even though the store is rather small, there are thousands of books neatly organized within its three long aisles. Wendy stops and sniffs the air.

"There's nothing like the smell of a million stories to welcome you to work, is there?" she asks, smiling with her eyes closed.

"I'm just happy the heater is on," I say, staring at a two-foot ceramic otter, perched on top of the register, holding a BOOK RECOMMENDATION jar. My dad probably made it. I immediately want to break it.

"All right. It's cash only. The register is self-explanatory, but if you do need anything, I'll be in the back doing paperwork."

"You're leaving me alone, just like that?" I ask.

"Rumor has it that you're a big boy. And if you get bored, read a book," she says, and heads to her office.

I'm starting to feel like picking up trash alongside the highway for community service wasn't such a bad option. It would suck, but at least I wouldn't die of boredom.

For the next hour I walk the aisles, pushing in any books that were out of place. It takes everything inside of me not to walk out and go hit up the casino. Gamblers have money. And they drink. I think of all the ways I might steal some cash from a drunk tourist tossing money around. Ugh. I just want to get this day over with so I'm one day closer to going back home.

I'm pacing back and forth in the fantasy section, trying to decide how I'll spend the next few hours, when I hear a jingle at the door. My first customer.

A family of four enters and begins their search for the perfect book. I head over to the register, so I can avoid them asking me any questions. The father walks to the history section, while the mother takes her two kids toward the children's section. I need to look busy. No one will approach me if I'm busy. I grab a pen and pull a sheet of paper from a notepad.

I'm doodling when the front door opens again. I look up, curious to see if it's someone mistaking this place for the casino or the church.

But the person who walks in is no gambler or nun. She

is, however, the strangest stranger I have ever laid my eyes on: a girl about my age. She moves like a dancer, walking to a beat only she can hear. Maybe she's from the church, doing some religious ritual I don't know about. A ritual where she has to hide her face. Because the top half of her face is hidden by a tightly fitted mask. It's so weird. Two eyeholes are cut out. It reminds me of Daredevil's mask, or Batman's, minus the pointy ears. It's solid black except for one yellow lightning bolt stitched onto the left side of it, above her eye. One could easily mistake her for an eccentric burglar, but who in their right mind would ever rob a bookstore?

The bottom half of her face is smooth and tan. Her skin, the color of those cinnamon sticks my mom puts in her coffee. And this girl's lips are as full and red as a blood moon. Her long black hair is tightly braided and hangs down like two sleeping snakes. She's definitely Native American. I wonder if she's Ojibwe. I wonder what's wrong with the rest of her face that she needs to hide it from the world. But mostly, I wonder why a girl that doesn't have to be in a bookstore would ever willingly come to one. She must be boring.

She wears a button-and-patch-covered denim jacket over a red hooded sweatshirt, Minnesota's signature camouflage pants, and big black leather boots. She's too far away for me to read most of the buttons and patches, but I do see a peace sign, a rainbow flag, and a button that looks like the earth.

She strolls directly to the children's section, where the mother and two kids take notice. I can't hear what they're saying, but the masked girl bends down and speaks to the kids, and two seconds later, the kids burst out laughing.

I want to get a closer look and maybe listen in, but as soon as I put down my pen, the father of the family approaches the counter and plops down a book on WWII battles.

"I'll take this," he says.

"Okay. How much is it?" I ask him. He raises an eyebrow.

"Nineteen ninety-five, I believe," he responds.

He pulls out his wallet but sets it down on the counter when he hears one of his kids call for him. He heads over and picks up his little girl.

While he's gone, the man's wallet stares at me, begging for my attention. I can see three twenty-dollar bills peeking out of it. Something very familiar inside of me wakes up. My blood heats. My heart beats like a drum. My hands sweat. And my brain is wondering why I haven't taken one of the twenties yet. Normally, it would happen so quickly, I'd barely notice. But I am here to stop stealing. Stealing is bad. But is it, really? In life, you can be a giver or a taker. And only a sucker gives. A survivor, like me, takes.

My mouth begins to salivate from the food I imagine I can get with half of that twenty-dollar bill. Okay. After this one time, I won't steal anymore. Maybe. This will be the last time. I promise myself. And if I break that promise, oh well, I'll just make another one . . . And before I finish my thought, my hand slides over to his wallet, and in one swoop, my fingers pluck one of the twenty-dollar bills from the billfold like an eagle plucks a fish from a lake.

Done.

I stuff it in my jeans pocket and go back to doodling, like it never happened.

The father returns with his daughter in tow. The little girl holds a small book about elephants in her hand. "This one too. And it's seven dollars," he says before I can ask him the price.

"Twenty-seven bucks," I say.

He reaches into his wallet and pulls out two twenty-dollar bills. He hands them to me, giving himself a brief look of confusion, before brushing it off.

I hit the cash button on the till and the drawer pops open. I hand the man a ten-dollar bill and three singles. And a nickel.

"Thanks," he says, grabs the books, and follows the rest of his family out the door.

A sheet of paper next to the register reads *Books sold* and has a list of titles along with the date of purchase and price. Maybe I should have written this transaction down. I pick up the pen and write in today's date and the prices before I forget them. Under title, I jot down *WW2 Book* and *Kids Elephant Book*.

As I close the cash drawer, I look up to see where the masked girl is. But she's gone. I walk around the desk and look into the aisles. She couldn't have left yet. I would have seen her, or at least heard the door jingle. Maybe she's a thief and stole a book. That would be awesome. Super nerdy, but awesome.

"I'll take this book," a voice says from behind me.

I turn around, and it's her. And for the first time, I see her eyes. They are light brown and have swirls of gold spiraling around her irises. "Hi," I say.

She responds by shoving the book into my chest and heading toward the register. That was rude. What's this girl's deal? And why does she wear that mask? Is it a weird northern Minnesota fashion trend to block the wind from half her face? Or is she disfigured? My curiosity is piqued.

I carry the book to the desk, but I don't stop staring at the mask. "Did you find what you were looking for?" I ask, trying to sound like an official employee.

"I'm afraid so," she says.

That's an odd response. And even though her voice is upbeat, I detect an attitude.

I finally look down at the book in my hand to see what she chose. It's a children's book. The kind for toddlers. There's a picture of a huge green caterpillar crawling across the cover of the book.

"Spoiler alert. This book ends with the little caterpillar turning into a butterfly," I say.

"You read it?" she asks.

"No. I just know how the world works," I say.

"Spoiler alert. This is how your world is going to work. You're the caterpillar, but instead of turning into a butterfly, you get plucked from the branch and end up in the belly of a bird . . . a jailbird, to be exact," she says, but I can't tell if she's smiling or being serious.

"I have no idea what any of that means," I say.

"I think you do."

"I think I don't," I snap back.

"Oh, I think you definitely do," she says, louder this time. She crosses her arms and tilts her head, daring me to continue this denial.

"What are you talking about?"

"I'm talking about you snaking that guy's cash just a minute ago," she says.

My stomach drops. How did she see that? I moved like a ninja. There's no way . . . Maybe I'm losing my touch after all.

"I don't know what you're talking about," I say, my voice weaker than I want it to be.

"Oh, so you're a liar too, huh? Wow. What a catch. I guess the only way to figure this out is to call the owner to review the footage," she says, and points to a camera mounted in the corner, aimed directly at us.

Oh crap. How did I not notice that camera? Wow. I really am getting careless.

"We don't need to go through all of that. Tell you what,

how about I break the twenty, give you half to keep you quiet, and we pretend it never happened?" I say.

"You see, the thing is, quiet really isn't my thing. I'm more of a turn-it-up-and-make-some-noise kinda girl. Besides, I don't want your blood money."

"Blood money?" I blurt out. "That's kinda dramatic."

"The guy worked hard for his money. With blood, sweat, and tears, so he can afford to bring his kids into bookstores and pick out an adventure to dive into before bed. You robbed him of that," she says.

"All right. Calm down. What do you want me to do about it?"

"I want you to ring me up so I can get out of here before you try to rob me."

"Well, to be fair, out of the two of us, it's you who looks like the robber in this situation, not me," I say, eyeing her mask.

"Don't judge a book by its cover."

"Or a girl by her mask?" I ask, trying to be funny.

"Ring me up and give me the twenty before that family pulls out of the parking lot," she says.

"Are you going to tell him I stole it?"

"I should, but if I did, he probably wouldn't come here again, and this place shouldn't suffer because of some sticky-fingered weasel like you."

"Weasel? It was just twenty bucks," I say and hand her the stolen bill.

"Now ring me up so I can get out of here," she says.

I ring her up. The book has a clearance sticker on it, stating 50 percent off the original price of sixteen dollars.

"Eight dollars." I hold out my hand.

"Oh, and you're going to pay for my book to keep me from ratting you out, got it?" she says.

"But you just said you weren't going to tell him I stole it," I say.

"As long as you cooperate. Now buy me this book," she insists.

I pull out some cash from my pocket. "If I'm buying you things already, shouldn't I at least know your name?"

"Who I am is not important. You should focus on who you are."

"I know who I am. I'm Benny. And this is Benny's eight dollars going into the register. There. I bought you a book," I say. "Need anything else?"

"I don't, but you do."

"Huh?"

"What you need is to wake up the superhero inside of you," she says.

I laugh. "Superhero? Inside of me? What the heck does that even mean?" I ask.

"You'll know soon enough." She takes her book and turns to walk out.

"Wait. Is that why you're wearing a mask? Captain Miss America?" I ask, laughing, as she reaches for the front door.

"See you around, thief," she says, and opens the door.

"Now who's judging a book by the cover? You just see a thief, huh?"

"Oh, no, you're much more than a thief. You're also the only person I've ever seen that can be surrounded by thousands of people, from thousands of years, from thousands of different places, different worlds even, and still find a way to be bored. You know what I call that kind of person?" she asks.

"A not-a-nerd?"

"Mamiidaawendam," she says.

Oh cool, sounds like another Ojibwe word. So, she is Ojibwe. Good to know.

"Does that mean I'm cute?" I ask, jokingly.

She releases the door, walks back to the register, snatches the pen off the desk, and writes it down. "You figure it out," she says, walks out, and approaches the family in the van.

I watch her speak to the man, who is in the driver's seat. She points to the floor and hands him the twenty-dollar bill. He thanks her and drives off. I rush over to the window to see if she heads toward the church or casino. She doesn't. Instead, she gets on a red bike propped up against the wall and rides down the street, until she is completely out of view.

Well, that girl hated me for sure. She even called me a "mommy-da-wendy" or something like that. How rude. Probably.

"I'm so hungry I could eat a cookbook," Wendy says from behind me.

I turn around and see her chewing, holding another bag

of chips. The lady is always eating. How is she in such great shape? Must be the hiking. And keeping up with three huge watch dogs all day.

"Did you see that girl who was just in here?" I ask.

"No. But I know everyone by the books they buy. What did she choose?" Wendy asks.

"A kid's book. About a caterpillar," I say.

She thinks and chews. "Hmmm. Could be anybody," she says, and walks toward the register. "People love caterpillars. I think because we all secretly hope to be butterflies one day. Wouldn't that be nice?"

"Nice? To be a bug? Nope. But you'd know this girl. She's hard to miss. She wears a mask over half her face."

Wendy shoots me a weird look. "A mask? Was she here to rob the store?"

"No, but she was kind of rude," I say.

"Come to think of it, I have heard little rumblings around town about a girl who wears a mask. Being an adult, I just assumed it was mere gossip," Wendy says as she counts the cash in the register.

"No, she's real," I say.

"Maybe I'll review the security footage to get a look at her," she says nonchalantly.

"That's okay. So, is it time to go home yet?" I ask, trying to distract her from the camera-related talk.

"Just about. Tommy has something special planned for you tonight," she says.

"What is it? Did he build me my very own jail cell in the garage?"

She laughs. "Not a bad idea, but no . . . He's taking you to a kind of tribal initiation thing," she says, and picks up the sheet of paper I was doodling on. "Mamiidaawendam," she reads aloud.

"You know what that means?" I ask excitedly.

"No. Did she call you this?"

"Yes. I'm sure it's not a very nice word."

"Well, ask your dad when we get home. He'll know. Come on, let's go." She closes the register, turns off the lights to the bookstore, and heads to the door.

We reach the Jeep just as the sun begins to fall behind the mountains. The casino parking lot is beginning to fill up. Car after car.

"I bet you wish your parking lot was as full as that one," I say.

"That place, my bookstore, and the church all have the same customers, just at different stages of their life," she says.

"I doubt that."

"Searchers, Benny. People searching for an escape. When they don't find it at one, they'll try the other. Sooner or later, they realize that all they need is a good book. And I'll be right there, ready to help them find it," Wendy says as she peels out of the parking lot and drives us home.

CHAPTER 8

HOW TO LAUGH AT LIFE

My dad is standing near the doorway holding up a bunch of neutral-colored fabrics with beads and feathers hanging down from them. His face looks serious. Wendy walks inside behind me and lets out a snicker. "What's all that?" I ask.

"Your outfit for tonight. It's traditional Ojibwe wear. I call it Ojibwear."

"I'm not Ojibwearing that. No Ojibway," I say.

"It is to honor your ancestors. Everyone will be wearing their family's symbols."

"You're in jeans and a LeBron James shirt," I say, pointing at his clothes.

"I've already honored my relations. I can wear whatever

I want now. But tonight is your night. Wewiib, get dressed." He shoves the outfit into my chest. "That means hurry up."

I grab it. This is going to suck. "Fine," I say. "I'll wear this goofy costume and please my sacred ancestors or whatever—"

"Stop talking. Start changing."

I march to the bathroom and shut the door behind me. I flip on the light switch and lay it out over the sink. There is a long-sleeve tan shirt with orange and yellow beads and painted lightning bolts and thunder cloud symbols on it, a brown leather fringed vest that goes over it, and a pair of beige pants that tie in the front. This looks like what white people wear on Halloween when they dress up as "Indians."

I remove my clothes and slip into the garments, avoiding the mirror. I don't want to see this until it's all put together. Like ripping off the scab in one quick swoop. After I put the shirt on, and the vest, I tie the pants tightly around my waist and stand in front of the mirror.

I look ridiculous. Perfect to play the "Native warrior" in one of those cheap cowboy movies, but in real life, right now, I look like a really bad joke. I sigh, thinking tonight is going to be super embarrassing. Why did I have to get the nice judge?

I open the door, and instead of laughing, my dad massages his nonexistent beard and looks me up and down. "You look good. Very authentic. But it's still missing something," he says as Wendy squeezes into the doorway to have a look.

She smiles and scratches at her also-nonexistent beard. "He needs neckwear," she says.

"Of course!" my dad says, and takes off down the hall. "Neck belts!"

"Don't give him ideas!" I say to Wendy, who can't keep a straight face.

"I know you want to, so go ahead and laugh," I say, and she uncorks her mouth and lets it all out.

"I'm not laughing at you, I'm laughing with you."

"But I'm not laughing."

"Okay. I'm laughing at you. Oops," she says in between her snorts.

My dad returns with three necklaces: one made from bone, one from wood, and one from stones and shells . . . and since he can't decide which one I should wear, he decides I'll wear all three. He drapes each one over my head, letting them rest on my chest.

"You like them?" he asks.

"I mean, maybe I should wear just one and not three?" I say.

"Nonsense. Would you rather have three dollars or one?" he says.

"Three, but—"

"Then it's settled. You wear all of them," he says, and clasps his hands together with satisfaction.

"He looks great, but not super great yet," Wendy says.

"Seriously?" I say.

"You're right . . . He needs more flair," my dad says, his eyes wide.

"Yes!" Wendy concurs. "We need everyone to see he means business. Big Bad Business Benny!"

"No! I am not wearing fringe or war paint or anything else," I protest, but they are already off and running to get more things to pile onto me.

Who refers to necklaces as neck belts? This is absurd. I should have stayed in Duluth. This isn't boot camp. This is a circus.

They return with globs of paint in their hands.

"Wait. Do I really have to wear this stuff? I mean, is it absolutely necessary?" I ask.

"You're not on vacation, Benny. You're here to work. Do chores. This isn't war paint. This is chore paint. Think of each color as community service," he says as he delivers the first smear of red paint under my eyes.

"And everyone is going to be all dressed up with painted faces?" I ask.

"Don't worry. You'll hardly be noticed," he assures me, even though that completely contradicts what he just previously said about me letting everyone know I mean business.

Wendy, with the black paint in one hand and the white paint in the other, follows suit. In a matter of seconds, I have twenty paint-covered fingers attacking my face. I close my eyes and take the punishment head-on. Do your worst. Fine. If everyone is going to look as silly as I am, then at least I'll blend in. They should call wherever I am going humiliation camp, not boot camp.

"Ta-da," Wendy says like a proud artist displaying her latest masterpiece.

I open my eyes and see them staring at me with huge matching grins on their unpainted faces. "You look . . . absolutely . . . ready," says my dad.

"Absolutely ready? That's it? Not absolutely kickass? Not ferocious? Not absolutely terrifying?" I say. "What happened to Big Bad Business Benny?"

"I mean, you're still scrawny, but we got to work with what we got. I bet you could scare a deer, maybe," he says.

"Or a porcupine," Wendy adds. "You'd scare the bejesus out of one of those, for sure."

"Can we go now? Or do you want to add a dozen feathers to my hair too?" I say, jokingly.

"You haven't earned your feathers yet, little bird," my dad replies solemnly.

Wendy pours a huge bag of dog food into three large tin bowls, all three labeled by their names: ROLEX, CASIO, and APPLE. Half of the food spills over onto the floor, but the dogs immediately begin cleanup detail, attacking the tiled floor first.

"Ambe," my dad says to me, grabbing his coat and tossing me an extra jacket of his. "That means 'let's go.'"

"You two have fun," Wendy says.

"You're not coming?" I ask.

"No, I'm staying in with George tonight. We might watch a movie if I can convince him to put the controller down.

"George, right. I haven't met him yet."

"He's not in the best of moods today. Maybe tomorrow?" For the first time I see sadness in her eyes.

"He's your son?"

"Yes. My shining star," she says, and looks up to the sky, like she can somehow see the stars through the roof.

"I'll explain some of that to you on the way," my dad says, and leads me out of the house.

The wind runs up and punches me in the face, then kicks me, then elbows me. I try to dodge its attack, but it's everywhere. Each strike feels like I was hit by a fistful of ice cubes.

"She's biting tonight. Get in," my dad says to me as I struggle with the door handle.

He reaches over and opens it for me. I climb inside and shut the door. "Duluth gets cold, but this is another level. Why do people willingly live here?" I ask.

"Coldness keeps you fresh. Those people in the lower states ain't as fresh as we are. It's like we're food. Minnesota is our fridge. Everybody else is just sitting on the counter, slowly spoiling. But not us," he says. "Remember that."

I never thought of it that way, and for good reason too.

Because it makes no sense! We're not food. Minnesota is not a refrigerator, and everyone else is not spoiling. Where does this guy get his logic from? "So, America is just one big kitchen, huh?" I say.

"It's a house. You got folks in California out on the porch, enjoying the sun. But the sun also ages you if you stay out too long. That's why they got so much plastic surgery over there. Minnesota wins. You got the people in the South out back, barbecuing and whatnot, but those mosquitoes will eat you alive. And the humidity keeps them upset all the time. Minnesota wins. You got the East Coast city folk in the bedroom always getting dressed up, always working, never sleeping. Those folks are always tired. Minnesota wins again. And then you got the whole center of America, eating fried everything, drinking, fighting, stockpiling all the guns. Now, those folks live in constant fear. Minnesota wins, yet again," he says.

"Everything you just said was a whole lot of ridiculousness," I say.

"True. But had you going, didn't I? I just made all that up on the spot. Impressive, huh?"

"No. Because you left out Florida."

"Floridians . . . We keep those folks in the basement," he says.

I'm laughing, which makes me angry. How weird is that? It feels wrong to be angry because I'm laughing. But I am. I'm angry that HE made me laugh. I'm angry that I let him and Wendy play dress-up with me. The only reason

I let them do it was because it slipped my mind that I was supposed to hate them. I forgot. How could I forget such an important thing? Now they'll think I'm their friend. Well, I'm not. Now they think what they did to me and my mom doesn't much matter because I'm smiling and laughing and appear to be fine. Well, I'm not. They must think I forgive them. Well, I don't. I never will.

I wipe the smile off my face and remember all the days and nights that I wished I had a dad. But mine left one day and never came back.

"Give it a try. What about the folks in Hawaii?" he asks.

"No thanks," I say, and turn my eyes toward the window. I bet he noticed the shift in my voice. I hope so. Let's just get this boot camp thingy over with so we can go our separate ways again

"Oh, I see. Still upset, are we? Okay. Be upset. Be a hard, impenetrable wall made of angry steel and furious concrete. But remember, every wall eventually comes down. And not always by sledgehammers and bulldozers, but sometimes by tiny forks of laughter and a spoonful of kindness, chipping away at it, day by day."

"Was that supposed to be profound? Tiny forks of laughter? Spoonful of . . . I mean, that was worse than your America-is-a-house thing," I say.

He reaches over and opens his glove compartment and pulls out a tiny fork. "Your wall will come down, Benjamin. I know this because I will not stop chipping away at it."

93

"You keep a tiny fork in your Jeep?" I ask.

"Doesn't everyone?" he says.

I immediately look away, forcing my eyes to the window again, because a smile almost formed on my face. Not that what he said was funny, but because of a memory that floated back to me. On one of our many drives from Duluth to Grand Portage, when I was small, we'd pack the car full of food because there weren't many stops on the way back then. In doing so, we'd always have our glove compartment full of spoons, forks, ketchup packets, and napkins.

"I guess I should tell you about George now," he says, sensing that I'm no longer willing to be in a happy-laughy mood.

"I don't really care one way or the other," I say, keeping my wall strong and intact.

"Wendy had a husband named Michael. Michael and Wendy have a son, George. He's twelve now. A year younger than you. When he was nine, his father took him camping. They'd go every summer, just the two of them. And one night, on their way home, they were hit by a drunk driver. Michael was killed instantly. George was injured and recovered after a few months of physical therapy. But mentally, he's still in bad shape. He hasn't left the house since. Won't go outside at all. Hardly ever leaves his room."

"Does he remember the crash?"

"He won't talk about it. He and his dad were very close.

Now the poor kid's terrified of everything. And angry," my dad says.

I can't imagine what life would be like not being able to go outside. Being afraid of everything. He probably relives the crash every night. I've seen enough movies to know that car accident victims are constantly haunted by the collisions. The grinding of steel on steel, mangled metal, shattered glass, the stuff of nightmares. No wonder he plays video games all day. That's all he really can do. That's probably the only time he sees daylight . . . through a blue-pixeled sky and a yellow digital sun.

"That sucks." I don't really know what else to say.

"As you can imagine, George is not a very happy kid anymore. It's been extremely tough with him, but it is slowly getting better. Day by day."

"Wendy seems okay, though. I mean, at least she seems happy," I say.

"Like anyone would, she too took it really hard. She lost her husband and her son's happiness. She was extremely depressed. She needed help. Around the same time, I was receiving help for my problems. That's where we met. And we've been each other's solid rocks ever since."

"You guys met at some rehab for damaged people?" I ask.

"What helped us is exactly what is going to help you," he says.

"The Native boot camp?" I ask.

"You can call it that if you like."

"It can't be too Native. I mean, if they let a . . ." I trail off.

"A white woman in? Do you believe a person who helps injured crows would refuse to help an injured pigeon? We were broken birds who needed help. Skin and feathers don't really matter much when the pain is the same."

I stare straight ahead at the road. "I've seen *Karate Kid*. Wax on, wax off. I don't need some old guy spilling all his wisdom onto me while I wash his car and walk his dog. I know stealing is technically wrong. Fighting is bad. Blah blah blah. I just do it because . . . I don't know. It's fun," I say.

"Fun. Well, look where all that fun landed you. Almost in juvenile hall. That sound fun?" he asks.

"No. But I'll be more careful next time."

"Sooner or later, you'll end up spending the rest of your life regretting there ever was a next time."

"What do you know about regret? You being a deadbeat worked out just fine for you. I mean, look, now you have a Wendy and a house and this Jeep, and you're, like, an artist now," I say, and don't even care that my tone has venom behind it.

"I regret what I put you and your mother through every single day of my life. But we can't change the past. All we can do is try to design our future and make sure we are better people than we were the day before."

"So that's why the whole house is designed to be some

walk-in vacation spot, right? George can't go to any of these places, so you bring those places to him?" I ask.

"Wendy and I try to encourage him by showing him what's out there awaiting him. The entire world."

"Well, from what I can see, it doesn't look like it's working."

"Nothing great happens overnight. These things take time."

"Why doesn't George just do the boot camp thingy?"

"George has to ask for help. That's how it works."

"I'm here and I didn't ask for help."

"Your mother asked for you."

"So, can't Wendy ask for George?"

"We've tried. George is still too angry. He needs to want the help. And before you say you don't want the help, ask yourself whether that's true," he says.

"I don't want the help, but I have to do it. It's court ordered, remember? So, I'll give the boot camp a try, but if someone tries to hypnotize me, I'm leaving. And they're not reading my palm, using tarot cards, or telling me stuff about my astrological sign," I say, setting my boundaries. "And no hippie meditation yoga either."

"We're here."

I imagined we'd be out in the middle of nowhere, surrounded completely by forest for some sacred tribal meeting. But nope, we have entered the parking lot of a large wooden building where a dozen other cars are parked, filling up over half the lot.

"Are we still in Grand Portage?" I ask.

"We are in Grand Marais now. I took you here once when you were five."

I don't remember this place at all. My dad parks the Jeep, and we step outside. It's still cold, but it's not beating me down the way it did earlier. Just the occasional slap in the face. As we get closer to the building, there is one thing that feels very Native American to this place. The music. The drums.

CHAPTER 9

NIIMI WAATESE

This place looks like the halls of a school, but instead of lockers on each side, lining the walls, there are dozens of pieces of artwork behind glass. Some are paintings, some are drawings, and some are photographs. Some are of animals, some of people, and some are beautiful illustrations of Lake Superior. I wonder who did all these? They look expensive, not that I can steal them. I wouldn't know the first thing about selling artwork. I follow my dad down the large hallway toward the red double doors. He stops in front of them and faces me.

"Is my punishment going to be drawing animals and taking pictures of trees and pretending I'm artistic?" I ask. "Because I'm not."

"This isn't boot camp. This is like a tribal council

meeting, to determine the difficulty level for your rehabilitation," he says, while holding back a smile.

"I had to dress up like this for a lame meeting?" I ask.

"Yes. First impressions are very important to our people," he says.

"Fine. Let's just get this over with."

"Now, remember, as you enter, make sure you're standing tall and proud. They sense fear, like wolves," he says.

"I think it's sharks who smell fear?" I ask.

"Then just swim in there like you own the ocean, okay?"

"Whatever," I say, and reach for the handle on one of the double doors.

"As you enter, say 'booni-wiisinig!' loudly, got it?" he says.

"What does it mean?"

"It means . . . umm . . . I am here for the sacred meeting," he says.

He stands back as I open the door, which makes a loud creak. Great, now I'm grabbing everyone's attention.

I push the door open, but to add excitement to my entrance, my dad kicks the other door wide open and pushes me forward, sending me a few feet into the room. The doors swing back, slamming shut behind me, leaving my dad in the hall. The drumming music abruptly stops.

I immediately feel the flames of humiliation engulf me. NO ONE IS DRESSED LIKE ME! There are dozens of people in here, and they have all stopped what they were doing and are looking at me like I set my body on fire. I see their eyes widening in disbelief as their jaws slowly drop. They are all dressed like everyday people, in jeans, shirts, and jackets. It just looks like your average gathering of people. And they're not even all Native American. At least I don't think they are. I see some white people and some Black people. I guess they can be Native American too, but some are as white as Wendy. What's going on here?

I whip my head back and see my dad through the tiny glass window slits. He gives me a thumbs-up. I want to murder him. I turn back to the crowd, not knowing what to do.

"Umm . . . booni-wiisinig," I say loudly, but not so proudly.

The entire room bursts into laughter.

The laughing gets louder. Some people have even collapsed at the sight of me, holding their stomachs, tears flowing. My dad finally enters and puts his hand on my shoulder. Not for comfort, but to hold himself up while he gets all his laughter out.

"Why would you do this to me?" I ask him.

"I had to make sure."

"Make sure what?" I ask.

"That you still have a sense of humor," he says. "Out with it. Laugh."

"What could possibly be funny about this? I look like a racist mascot!"

The crowd laughs. How do they find this funny?

101

"Brothers and sisters, friends and neighbors, I give you my son, Benjamin Waterfalls!" he shouts to the hysterical crowd.

"What did I say to them just now?" I ask.

"Stop eating, you people!" he says.

The crowd wipes their tears away and applauds. I don't get it. Why are they all clapping? I didn't do anything besides stumble in like a clown and stare at them. Interestingly enough, they all did stop eating—momentarily.

"Love the costume, bro, you're hilarious," one teenage girl says to me, and gives my dad a welcoming hug.

She's not in a costume. She's in a leather jacket and cargo pants.

I look at my dad. "This isn't traditional Native American wear, is it?"

"The 'Made in China' tag didn't give it away, huh?" he replies, which causes both of them to laugh again.

I reach back behind my neck and feel the tag. One yank, and it's in my hand, and sure enough, it reads MADE IN CHINA.

"Or the fact that all those beads on your vest are plastic?" the teenage girl says.

"And who are you?" I ask.

"I'm Opichi Kenosha. It means Robin. You can call me either one," she says, and now gives me a hug.

"Um, okay . . . Hi, Either One," I say.

She laughs. "I met you when you were still in diapers. We're family. It's good to see you all grown up," Robin says. "I got to head out. Got a gig down in Duluth. Have a fun trip," she says to me and leaves the room.

There was my shot at getting back to Duluth. I could have begged her for a ride. And what did she mean, "have a fun trip"? I'm stuck here. She's the one leaving . . . But it makes sense when she opens the exit door, because I get a glimpse of the back of her jacket. It reads LIFE'S A TRIP. I don't know how we're related, but I bet I looked less ridiculous in diapers than I do now.

My dad had been holding my jacket. I grab it and put it back on. I can't hide the whole outfit, or my Skittles-painted face, but I can at least avoid the cold draft in here. I zip it up, and a whole crowd of people approach us.

I watch them all hug my dad first. They speak Ojibwe to him, and it trips me out that he answers back. I keep hearing the word *boozhoo*. I used to know that one. I think it means "hello," but I blocked it out of my mind when my dad started drinking because it sounds like *booze*. I hated the word after that. I forgot it on purpose. Now it's being tossed around by everyone. After a few women hug me and squeeze my cheeks, telling me how cute I am, I see an opening and walk toward the table full of snacks. Being humiliated sure works up an appetite.

I grab a Rice Krispies treat and eat it while picking up

two brownies and a root beer. I make sure no one is looking and slip a few extra Rice Krispies treats into my coat pocket for later.

"You don't have to steal them. They're free," a voice says from behind me.

I turn around. It's the girl from the bookstore. She's dressed in a long yellow coat, black jeans, and heavy boots. She's still wearing the lightning bolt mask tightly fitted over her face.

"Well, if it isn't Captain Native America," I say. "Are you following me?"

"You sound paranoid. But most thieves are, aren't they?" she says.

I should return fire with a quick and witty comeback, but instead I watch her. She picks up a Rice Krispies treat and takes a bite. Her teeth are as white as clouds. Whatever the issue is with her face, her teeth look healthy. And why am I staring at her lips? I move my eyes upward.

"Seriously, though, why are you wearing that mask?" I ask.

"We all wear masks, Benjamin. Even you," she says, and takes another bite.

"Oh, all this paint on my face? No. This was my dad's prank. Wait. How do you know my name?" I ask.

"Aren't you Big Bad Business Benny?" she asks.

"Wow. Word spreads fast around here. And yeah, I'm supposed to have a meeting to determine how rotten of a person I am. It's probably a scam, though."

"A scam? You sound paranoid and skeptical."

"I just want to get this all over with so I can go back home and resume my life," I say.

"Your life is that awesome, huh?" she asks.

"It is what it is."

"It is what it is? Wow. So profound. You come up with that all by yourself?" she asks.

"It's the truth. Sometimes life kicks butt. And sometimes life kicks you in the butt. Oh, no, I'm sounding like my dad."

"Your dad. Tommy. He's a really good guy," she says.

I laugh. "Well, you must not know him very well."

"Because he left you and your mother?"

"Jeez. Does everyone know everyone's business around here?" I ask.

"The Grand Parents are small places. Everyone is family around here," she says.

"The Grand Parents?"

"Yeah. Grandma Marais and Grandpa Portage," she says.

"Ah, got it. Nice that you got wordplay this far north."

"We got it all up here. Word is, we even got a thief now."

"Hopefully for not very long. I plan on leaving as soon as I can," I say.

"Well, there's one thing you can't steal . . . Time. You'll be here for as long as it takes." She turns and starts to walk off.

"Wait. Can I at least know your name? Since everyone already knows mine," I say.

She sighs. "I am Niimi Waatese."

"Wow. You can't get more Ojibwe than that, can you?" I ask. "What does that mean?"

"She is dancing, there is lightning." She does a quick little dance move, then slams her hands together like a quick little lightning strike and walks off again, this time disappearing into the mingling crowd.

Niimi Waatese. Her name is a sentence. That's kind of cool. And the other girl I met was named Robin. I wonder why? Was a robin around when she was born? Did she enter the world crying so beautifully it sounded like the singing of a bird? Is she destined to fly? How do Native Americans get their names? I really don't know much about my own people. My friends back in Duluth have boring white names like Bryan and David. Benjamin is not very Native sounding either, but at least I have my last name. Waterfalls. That always felt Native to me. Niimi is lightning and I'm a waterfall. And a bird just hugged me. This is an interesting night already.

Why does Niimi wear that mask? I shouldn't care. I'm not here to make friends, especially not ones that wear masks. I just need to meet with this council, pretend to listen to what they say, and get this boot camp thing underway. Pretending to be rehabilitated is almost as good as being rehabilitated, right?

A man in the front of the room clasps his hands together, grabbing everyone's attention. He takes the center of the room and speaks. He must be the chief. He has long black hair, sitting under a black baseball cap. His skin is as tan as my dad's, but he dresses better. He dresses like he's on stage at a concert, in dark jeans, a white T-shirt, and a leather jacket. His face is kind and strong. And not a trace of facial hair on it. I wonder if he has to shave every day. His rock and roll shirt and jeans completely destroy the image in my head of what Native American chiefs are supposed to look like. If he was in Hollywood auditioning for the role of a chief, he'd be rejected. Which is crazy because he's an actual chief. I squint at the logo on his colorful shirt. It's of the band A Tribe Called Red. Wow. What a cool chief. They're huge in Duluth.

"Aaniin!" he says to the crowd of people.

I look at my dad, who stands directly behind me. He's smiling. I'm not.

"Greetings," my dad whispers to me, even though I didn't ask.

"Tonight is a special night. One of our own has returned. He is here to bloom," he says.

The crowd applauds. Bloom? What does that even mean? And why are they clapping? They don't even know me, and they're already rooting for me. They should boo me and toss me out of here. But instead, they're all pretending to care about me. Why?

"But before we get to him, I must warn you, gimood-ishki," he says. "So hide your wallets and purses."

The crowd laughs and heads start to turn toward me. My dad leans in and says, "It means 'he is a thief.'"

No wonder the people next to me took one step back.

"Before we meet the young misakakojish, I want someone else to speak with you all. As many of you know, niwiiw, my wife, my aki, recently left this world."

The group nods, sad eyes all around. That sucks. The dude's wife died. I wonder if she looked like a rock star too.

"She and I worked closely together on making our community the best it can be for all of us. With her gone, I've seen dark, heavy days and sleepless nights. I reached out for help. I reached out for a light to my darkness. Indaanis," the chief continues.

"That means my daughter," my dad says into my ear.

"Ever since she was knee-high, she's been helping her mother bloom our community. She has been there every time I have been there for you," he says, and the crowd nods.

"And as your traditional tribal leader, my responsibility is to do what is best for all of you. These are strange times for us all. I am here today to announce to you all that I, Chief Waatese, have begun training my daughter, Niimi Waatese, to be the head of the Gichigami Garden, where she will be leading all future bloomings."

The crowd gasps. Some cheer, some do not.

"But she's too young!" a woman shouts.

"Yes, Miakoda, she is young. But it is the youth that will lead us to healing. The youth will replace us. The youth will be in charge of this aki when we are gone. And those who know her know no one is better suited for the job. Niimi has left school to focus on her training. She will be here for all of you."

"Are you saying she will be our ogimaakwe?" an elder woman asks.

"One day, I hope so. But for now, I will remain Ogimaa. My focus will be to assist in government affairs, language programs, health programs, and ceremonies," he says to the crowd.

"Isn't she a bit . . . too out there to handle the bloomings?" an older man speaks up.

A few in the crowd laugh. I don't know what's funny. I also have no clue what bloomings are. And what the heck is a Gichigami Garden?

"I will be the first to admit, her methods, as were her mother's, are a bit unconventional, but many of you have already witnessed the medicine she carries," he says.

Then it hits me. He said Niimi Waatese. The girl in the mask. That's his daughter. She's going to be the head of something and one day possibly be the new chief? Are tribal leaders allowed to dress up as superheroes and buy children's books?

"We all mourn your wife," another man says. "We loved her, and we love your daughter, but putting a child in charge of something so important is, perhaps, not the best answer, especially in today's world."

"The best answer can only be given if the best question is asked. And I challenge you to ask Niimi all of your best questions. I open the floor to you all. I raised her, yes, but it is every day that she teaches me about this ever-changing world."

Niimi walks through the crowd and approaches her father. The way the crowd parts, it's obvious they all have respect for her. But I can see some are not yet convinced she is ready for the role. I wish I could see the rest of her face so I could get a sense of how this is all going down with her.

Then she speaks.

"Aaniin. I understand your hesitance. I too was hesitant when my father approached me about this. The thought of being taken out of school scared me. But the more I thought about it, the more sense it made. The one who blooms people should be young, in order to grow and adapt to this unpredictable world. I will bring new ideas and new perspectives to all the challenges we face today and tomorrow. I look at you all, many of whom I have already had the pleasure of seeing bloom. Like you, Namid Morrison. When you lost your art gallery to the heavy rains and had nowhere to turn, who kept you focused? Who led a fundraiser to help you rebuild? Who sat with you every night, not letting you give up, and made sure you created more art?"

"You and your father did," says Namid, an older woman who is dressed in a fringed vest and bell-bottoms, like she's stuck in the 1960s.

"That's right. And look at you now. I doubt there's a person in here that doesn't have one of your paintings hanging on their wall," Niimi says.

Is she the artist who did all the paintings in the hallway?

"And you, Mr. LeSage, when you lost your job at the refinery and you wanted to give up, feeling too old to start over, who convinced you to go back to school and learn a new trade?"

A tall, broad-shouldered man steps forward. "You and your mother did."

"And at fifty-three years old, you start this year as a nurse's aide, correct?"

"That's correct. I'm an official healer," he says.

The crowd applauds.

"Yes. I am young, and to put your trust in me is asking a lot, I get that. But isn't that the whole point of trust? If it was easy to give, it would be worthless. We face great challenges, and the only way to meet those challenges, and defeat them, is by thinking outside the box. So, I stand here, proudly, alongside imbaabaa, as your friend, your sister, and your Gichigami gardener, Niimi Waatese."

After a few random claps, the room gives in and delivers a thunderous applause.

"And now, I'd like to welcome the sneaky little misaka-kojish to join me up here. His blood is Ojibwe, but his heart has a large white hole in it. He tries to fill it by stealing things. Stuffing them into his broken heart, but this hole only grows deeper and wider and hungrier. We need to fill it with the only thing a heart needs . . . his blood. And we are his blood. So, Benjamin Waterfalls, the son of Tommy Waterfalls, you sneaky little badger, please step forward." The crowd parts, giving me an open lane toward Niimi.

This is awkward. I don't move until my dad elbow-nudges me forward. Slowly, I approach Niimi. With her twirling finger, she signals me to turn around and face the crowd. So, I do. Gulp. All eyes on me. I don't know which is worse, being humiliated by showing up to this place looking like a five-dollar Halloweendian or being forced into public speaking. I hate being stared at. I'm a thief. I literally rely on not having attention on me.

"Daga," she says.

Ha. I know that one. "Please what?" I ask.

"Speak."

What does she want me to say? I don't know any of these people. I don't live in this world. I just want to go home. Heck, I'll even go back to the bookstore if it gets me out of this room.

"Hey," I say to the crowd.

"Boozhoo!" they shout back to me.

Ugh. There's that word again. *Boozhoo*. Booze, who? Whose booze? My dad's. He's a drunk. He is the reason I'm here. This is all his fault. I look at him and hope he feels every dagger my eyes are shooting toward him.

"You have to open your mouth to speak. Like how I'm doing right now," Niimi says, and the room laughs again.

"Well," I say, "I'm not sure what to tell you. I'm a thief, I guess. But you should know that Miss Bloom Girl over here just bought a kid's book about caterpillars today. Recommended reading age was three to six years old. Good luck with her as the head of the tribe someday."

The crowd laughs. But I wasn't joking. Even my dad is laughing. And Niimi and her dad are laughing too.

"He's quite the aadizookewinini, isn't he?" Niimi says to the crowd.

They laugh again. "What's that mean?" I ask her. "What did you just call me?"

"I called you a storyteller. And that's a good thing, Benny. Most people with holes in their hearts decide to give up. They believe the whole world gave up on them, when in reality, it was they who gave up on the world. But you, you steal and tell yourself stories about how it's not your fault. Never your fault. Always someone else's, am I right?" she asks in front of everyone.

"It's his fault," I say, and point to my dad.

The crowd clasps their hands together, like Niimi just did something amazing, but she didn't. I'm just telling the truth.

"This is a girl who wears a mask, but she's no superhero. She's not even that nice. And my dad isn't some sweet and kind man that you all think he is. I'm out of here," I say, and start to walk out of the now-very-silent room.

"Everything you're feeling is right on schedule, Benny," Niimi says.

I stop. "You don't know me," I say, and try to kick the double doors open. But they open the other way. It's *pull*, not push, so I look like a crash test dummy that just kicked a closed door and nearly slammed my body into it from the momentum.

"Life is give and take, but doors are push or pull. To open them, you must first—"

"Oh, shut up! You're not wise. You're just a kid, like me. And us kids are full of mistakes. You shouldn't be the head of anything. In fact, it was a mistake coming here. You can all go bloom yourselves!" I shout, and open the door and begin to walk out.

"Do we have a winner?" Niimi asks the crowd.

An old woman who looks nearly a hundred raises her hand. I stop to see what the heck is going on. A winner? For what?

"Mrs. Cloquet, what did you have?" Niimi asks.

Mrs. Cloquet pulls out a small folded sheet of paper, unfolds it, and reads, "Shut up. You're not wise. You're just an old man. It was a mistake coming here," she says, and looks up at Niimi. "I thought he'd be speaking to your father, though."

"Close enough. You win," Niimi says.

The crowd applauds.

"But I did like his improvisations. I really liked the you-guys-can-go-bloom-yourselves bit," Mrs. Cloquet adds. "He's very clever."

The room laughs again. "It should be a bumper sticker," another man adds.

"Is everything funny to you people?" I shout.

"You people?" Niimi asks, which causes the crowd to go silent.

"I obviously didn't mean it like that," I say.

"How'd you mean it?" Niimi asks.

"I just mean . . . I don't know. Not everything is funny. Life isn't. Sometimes it really sucks," I say on my way out of there. "Like right now."

Niimi's father finally speaks. "Life is a story, Benny. You get to choose what kind. Ojibwe humor is rooted back to the very first Anishinaabe man and woman. When we first began to speak. Our first words weren't 'wow, we can talk' or 'are you hungry' or 'good morning.' Our first words were a riddle. Would you like to know the riddle?" he asks me.

"No. I'm done with all your jokes," I yell.

"We've experienced enough tragedies. It's time to choose to make life a comedy. Isn't it funny that we're all alive on a spinning rock, hurtling through space, while dressed up in our skin and bones, trying to understand the meaning to our existence? Life is a riddle. And we'll laugh as we try to figure it all out all the way to the next world," he says.

115

"Did you laugh when your wife died?" I ask, and hurry through the hallway toward the parking lot before he can respond.

I can't believe I just asked him that. I feel awful. Of course he didn't laugh. He'd already expressed how difficult life is without her. What's wrong with me? And Niimi . . . If she didn't hate me already, she most certainly does now.

I brush the guilt away. It's their fault for trying to make life sound like a sitcom. Life isn't funny. It isn't a riddle. It's a take-what-you-can-get-before-you're-dead kind of world. I just want to get this boot camp started so I can go back to Duluth.

In the hallway, a glass display holding a bunch of art catches my eye. Not so much the actual art, but my reflection from the glass. They planned all of this. My appearance. My outburst. Everything. They just wanted to humiliate me. Of course, they were all laughing. Why wouldn't they? I look hilarious.

What kind of boot camp is this?

I'm done!

CHAPTER 10

LIGHTNING DANCER

I wish I was there to see it," Wendy says as soon as I walk through the door.

"Yeah. I was a hit." I walk past Hawaii. I just want to change, wash my face, and go to sleep.

"How was the food?" she asks. "Did you bring any back?"

"No, sorry," I lie.

"Where's Tommy?" she asks.

"He's right behind me. But I don't want to talk to him. And I don't really want to talk to you, either. You let me walk right into that trap," I say, and head toward the bathroom.

"Aren't you going to ask how my night was?"

"No."

"Well, George and I had pizza, and I watched him play—"

"Wendy. You're not my family," I say. "In fact, you're the opposite of my family. You judge me for being a thief, but you're the biggest thief of all. You stole my dad." I slam the bathroom door.

The mirror looks back at me. I can't believe I was seen in public like this. I splash water over my face, and the sink fills with painted water. As the liquid swirls down the drain, so do my words to Wendy.

I don't know why I was so mean to her. I don't know why I was so mean to Niimi's dad either. What's happening to me? I thought this place was supposed to make me feel better. I feel worse. And I don't want to face these feelings. Feelings are for crybabies. I need to sleep. That's all. I scrub my face, hoping to remove the paint and these annoying emotions.

There's a knock on the door. I dry off and swing it open. "Living room. Now," my dad says, and walks away.

This is not good.

Tommy and Wendy are waiting for me in the living room. Right outside Jamaica, which puts them somewhere in the carpeted sea. Wendy stares at me, both lips tucked into her mouth. I know that look. My mom does it too when she has something to say but is waiting for the right moment. My dad reaches out and takes Wendy's hand. His eyes are wide, lips pursed, making dozens of little ripples around his mouth, "You have something to say?" he asks me.

"I do if you do," I say to him.

"Excuse me?" he asks.

"After what you just put me through, you want me to apologize? How about you apologize for once in your life? You made me look like a complete fool in front of all those people. You let them all laugh at me and call me a thief!"

"I must have gotten all my information wrong. So, you're not a thief?" he asks sarcastically.

"That's not the point," I interject.

"That is precisely the point. That's the only reason why you were there tonight. Dressing you up and putting all the paint on your face was to keep your mind off hating me for a few minutes. You've hated me since the moment you arrived. I needed to distract you from that anger. If I hadn't done it, there was a very slim chance of even convincing you to go."

"Oh, so I should be thanking you?" I ask.

"No. I want you to stop thinking about yourself as the victim for once and start thinking about what you said to Wendy," he says.

I look at Wendy. She may look tough, but I see that she wants to cry.

"Sorry, Wendy," I say.

"Sorry for what?" she asks.

Great. She's milking the moment. "I shouldn't have said what I said, but I said it and you heard it and I can't unsay it and you can't unhear it so all I can say is I'm sorry. You happy now?" And I dive my hands into my pockets while keeping my eyes on anything but her.

Jeez. They were just words. Get over it.

"But you can unsay it and I can unhear it," she says to me, her pained eyes brightening with blue excitement.

"Really? You own a time machine?" I ask.

"Everyone has one. Wanna see it?" she asks.

"Another stupid game. Sure."

"Go outside. Come back in. Boom. That's my time machine. Hurry up."

I look at my dad, but he's smiling at her. He likes what she just said, even though we both know it's complete madness. "Now," she reminds me.

I can't believe she wants me to do this. Role play. Two adults wanting me to pretend. Fine. I already played dress-up with them. I walk past them and open the door, and as I shut it, my dad grabs the handle. "Wait for me. I was out there with you," he says.

My dad joins me outside. It's just me and him and him and me. I take a deep breath and reach for the door, but my dad lifts his arm up, signaling me to wait.

"What?" I ask.

"Give her a minute. She needs to get into character," he says.

"Character? She just playing herself . . . From literally two minutes ago," I say.

"Going back in time two minutes, or two hundred years, still takes focus. Focus takes time. She takes these roles seriously. She took theater in high school. Let her become the Wendy of minutes two past," he says.

"When you say things like that, you really don't hear how bonkers you sound, do you?" I ask.

"What's the matter? Is the thief afraid of Wendy stealing the scene?" he asks, and nudges his finger into my chest.

"There is no scene. I'm only here because the judge forced me to be here. These little games may be fun for you and Wendy, but they're not for me. Do you understand that?" I ask.

"The judge forced you, huh? That reminds me of a joke I know. Wanna hear it?" he asks, and suddenly I think he just wants to keep me out here for some weird alone time. He'll even attempt to make up a joke on the spot. It won't be funny, but that's not the point. He just wants to cram my many years of hating him together and replace it with a two-minute bonding session. Well, guess what? Not happening.

"No," I say, and reach for the door, but he lifts his finger—so I stop—ugh. I don't know why that finger thingy still works on me.

"When the thief got caught, the judge was forced to give him a very long sentence because of what the thief stole from him . . . Now, what did the thief steal?"

"That's a riddle, not a joke," I say.

"What did the thief steal?"

121

"I give up."

"All the punctuation keys from his keyboard," he says, and laughs. "Get it? Without them, he's forced to give long sentences."

He stops laughing when he sees that I'm not amused.

"Can I go in now?"

"I'm waiting on you. Wendy's always ready," he says.

Ugh. He's so frustrating. I open the door and enter. And just like she was, Wendy greets me as I enter. Or reenter. Whatever. This time my dad follows closely behind me, probably to make sure I don't screw this up again.

"How did it go?" Wendy asks happily.

"Oh, hi, Wendy. It was amazing. The stunt you and my dad pulled by making me dress up like a super-offensive cosplay Indian was a smash. Everyone laughed at me. It was great. How was your night?" I say.

She smiles. "It was pretty good. George and I had pizza, and I watched him shoot a bunch of zombies that tried to invade his military compound. Thanks for asking," she says.

"Okay. Well . . . I guess that's it," I say, and walk past her.

"Wait," she says.

I turn around. "What! Did I not do it good enough?" I ask.

"You were great. I was just going to tell you that there's still some pizza left. Are you hungry?" she asks.

I am hungry. So hungry. All I had today was half a grilled

cheese, two brownies, and three small Rice Krispies treats. "Really? Yes. I'd love some pizza."

"Great. Why don't you change first. You look ridiculous. Then come back for some grub. George promised to meet you when you got home, so try not to look like a zombie . . . Or he'll likely kill you," she says jokingly.

"Okay," I say, and retreat into the garage to change.

The fluorescent lights flicker on. All three dogs are sleeping on my bed, taking up the entire mattress. Great. My bed is going to smell like dog. I slip into a pair of sweatpants and my favorite oversize purple hoodie. I don't remember where I got it, but it's by far the most comfortable article of clothing I own. I sleep in it almost every night, which explains why it's so faded. My mom said there was a Vikings logo on it once, but ever since I can remember, it's just been a purple hoodie. Now that I'm older, it's still big on me, but I'm no longer swimming in it.

The thought of pizza quickens my feet back into the main part of the house. I hope there's a lot left over. I can usually eat a whole pizza by myself.

As I step into the living room, I see George. And he sees me. We just stare at each other. My dad and Wendy watch us lock eyes like we are two lions waiting for one to make the first move.

"Hey, that's my hoodie," my dad says. "I haven't seen that in years."

Now I want to burn it.

George is taller than me, and what I didn't notice in his dark bedroom is his skin is much darker than mine. His hair is very short and black, but there is a white streak in it, as if a small part of his head thinks it is time to be an old man. He wears a white thermal shirt under his blue Minnesota Timberwolves tee. And red plaid pajama bottoms cover his long legs.

"You're Black?" I blurt out.

I didn't see that coming, and sometimes when I'm caught off guard, I speak with no filter.

"Thanks for letting me know," he says. "I had no idea."

"George, this is Benny. Benny this is my son, George," Wendy says.

"He's ugly," George says, which sneaks out a snicker from my dad.

"He's not that ugly," Wendy says.

"It just looks that way because he's in a house full of super-attractive people. Trust me, outside in the world, he's average-looking," my dad adds.

Oh, awesome. More jokes. I bet Grand Portage is the birthplace of all comedians.

"I hear you're going to be staying here for a little bit. Apparently, I had no say in it, but I do have one rule . . . My room is off-limits. You don't go in there," George says to me. "Understand?"

"I don't know how much they told you about me, so I'm

going to let you in on a little secret . . . I don't follow rules very well. In fact, I've already been in your room," I say.

His eyes widen, then dance over to Wendy and back to me. "Yeah, right," he says.

"You were playing your video game. You didn't even notice me in there. I could have taken whatever I wanted while you were shooting zombies," I say.

He looks pissed. Maybe I shouldn't have started it off this way, but one thing I can't stand is someone my own age trying to give me rules. Especially a nerd.

"You touch my stuff, and I'll punch you in the face," he says.

"Fellas . . ." My dad steps in. "There will be no punching in this house."

"How you going to punch me if you can't catch me? I mean, all I got to do is take a step outside, right?" I say.

His eyes shoot to Wendy. "You told him!"

"I didn't say—" she starts.

"I met him! There! You happy? If he comes into my room again, I'm going to stuff him into a suitcase and leave him by the door. In fact, all of you stay out of my room!" George says, and walks back to his bedroom.

The door slams loudly, which causes Wendy to jump. "That went well," I say.

"Why did you say that to him, Benny?" my dad asks.

"Obviously, so he'd do what he just did," I say.

"And why did you want him to do that?" Wendy asks.

"Easy. More pizza for me." I grab two slices off the coffee table. They're not hot anymore, but warm pizza is almost as good as hot pizza. In fact, cold pizza is almost as good as warm pizza. The only pizza I don't like is no pizza. I start walking back toward the garage.

"Benny," Wendy says.

I stop and turn to her as I take my first bite.

"You didn't have to do that." She sighs and walks out of the room.

I look at my dad, who bites his bottom lip and sighs. "I know why you said it."

"Oh, yeah, enlighten me," I say.

"Hurt people hurt people," he says, and walks off to join Wendy.

Hurt people hurt people. What does that even mean? I'm not hurt. I'm hungry. They're totally different.

I slink back into the garage and try to sit on the bed. Half of my butt leans off it because of the three giant watch dogs. And ugh. They are snoring. Loudly too. I don't care that I upset George. It's his fault. He shouldn't try to lay down the law on someone he doesn't even know. But . . . I managed to hurt Wendy's feelings multiple times today, even though she's probably the nicest one in the house. My dad must really like sensitive women. My mom is the same way.

I break up the last few bites of pizza into three chunks and place one in each dog bed. All three watch dogs get up and take the bait. Haha. I got my bed back. I lie down and grab the piece of folded paper that Niimi gave me at the bookstore. I unfold it and read it: *Mamiidaawendam*. I try to pronounce it to myself. I wonder what it means?

I can ask my dad, but I don't want him thinking I need his help. So I tiptoe to my Dad's office, and am relieved that I can get on his laptop without a password. I search the internet for the definition. After I've misspelled it twice, the search results find one definition. Ha! There's an actual Ojibwe to English translation site. That will come in handy around here. I read the translation and laugh. *Mamiidaawendam: He who has a troubled mind.*

Really? I have the troubled mind? My dad can't stop telling unfunny jokes to save his life, Wendy is an always hungry female version of him, George is afraid to step outside, and the entire Grand Portage tribe of Ojibwe are going to be bloomed by a twelve-year-old girl who wears a mask. And what the hell does blooming people even mean? Flowers bloom. People don't. I'm probably the least "troubled mind" out of everyone here. Including these three loud, smelly dogs.

Before I close the laptop, I see several emails from my mom to my dad, with "Benny?" in the message lines. I know she's worried, but I'm still mad at her for sending me here. She can worry a bit longer.

CHAPTER 11

I MAKE SUPERHEROES

Splash! Water hits my face. I launch out of sleep and out of bed, drenched and confused. Niimi stands before me, holding a dripping red bucket. She's wearing denim overalls today, and a white thermal shirt under them. I still can't see all of her face because of the mask, but I see her smile. Normally smiles are contagious and make you smile back at them, but this girl just dumped a bucket of water on me, so I am definitely not smiling.

"Are you out of your mind?" I shout.

"Some have said so, but we're running late, so I had to think quickly," she says.

"Right. Instead of just waking me up like a normal person, you went and found a bucket, filled it with water, and dumped it on me. You do know that takes much longer than just 'hey, wake up,' right?"

"Yes. That's why we're running late. I couldn't find the bucket right away. You ready?"

This girl makes no sense. I have some serious concerns for the tribe if she's going to be the one running it someday. "Ready for what?" I ask.

"You're working with me today. Chomp-chomp! Put these on," she says, and picks up a folded stack of clothes, shoving it into my chest.

"It's chop-chop, not chomp-chomp."

"Have you had breakfast yet?" she asks.

"Obviously not. You just woke me up."

"Then it's chomp-chomp. Like you're chewing. After breakfast it's chop-chop."

"Whatever. There's no arguing with someone like you," I say.

"Now you're learning. I'll be waiting in Jamaica. It's warmer there," she says, and walks out of the garage.

I look at what she picked out for me to wear: the black long-sleeve shirt my mom got me for my twelfth birthday, with a picture of a cat in an astronaut suit floating in space with the caption ASTROCAT written in neon green graffiti across it. It's one of my favorites. I slap on my jeans and my black hoodie, put on my shoes, and notice all three dogs staring at me. Well, they are actually staring at my bed.

"Fine. But don't slobber on it," I say, and all three dogs jump out from their dog beds and pile onto mine. Watch dogs. More like watch-me-sleep dogs.

I exit the garage and rush over to the bathroom to pee and brush my teeth. After the pizza, Rice Krispies treats, grilled cheese, and brownies, I feel like my teeth are wearing sweaters.

I never actually agreed to hang out with Niimi, but if it gets this boot camp thing rolling, I'm in. I'm actually pretty excited to finally do something. Even if it's labor. I just need to feel like this is all going somewhere. I have decided that I will even forget how mad I am at Niimi for taking part in my humiliation initiation last night.

My dad and Wendy are having breakfast at the table. The smell of waffles floats toward me. Niimi is not standing in Jamaica. She must have switched travel plans . . . She's in Scotland.

"Good morning," Wendy says to me, and hands me a golden, buttery waffle.

I take it and shove it into my mouth and muffle out "good morning" back to her.

"You and Niimi got an interesting case today. Should be fun," my dad says.

"Case? What is she, a detective?" I ask.

"Aren't we all," he says, and chews. "We're always searching for clues. But Niimi is gifted. She finds people who don't know they're lost."

"She looks lost." I point to her as she stands in Scotland, balancing on one leg as she tries to fit into a kilt that was hanging on the Scottish shelf.

"You think if I stand in here long enough, I'll develop a Scottish accent?" she asks.

I turn back to Wendy and my dad. "See what I mean?"

"Never thought about that. I'll give it a try and hang out in France today. I really need to brush up on *Moi Francois*," Wendy says to her.

I roll my eyes.

My dad laughs. "Don't pretend to have the world all figured out, Benny. You'll close yourself off from all the magic that comes your way."

"There's no such thing as magic," I reply.

"People said the same thing about lightning before they saw it," Niimi says. "No matter how unlikely it sounds, bolts of electricity do shoot down from the skies. The only people who get struck by it are those who stay outside during the storm, refusing to believe it's real."

"Spoken like a true ogimaakwe," my dad says as they fist-bump.

"No. Lightning is real because it's proven by science. Magic is made up for fairy tales and movies and books," I say.

"And where do you think fairy tales, movies, and books come from?" Niimi asks me.

"From people," I reply.

"And are those people real?" she asks.

"Obviously."

"Interesting," my dad says, biting into another waffle.

"No. Not interesting," I snap. "It's called imagination. You think it up and write it down, but that doesn't make it real."

"Isaac Newton, Galileo, and Einstein thought up some pretty imaginative ideas and wrote them down. I guess gravity is not real to you?" Niimi asks me.

"Interesting," Wendy says.

"Not interesting! That's different," I say.

"Just think about how silly the Left Sisters were, or is it the Wright brothers?" Niimi ponders aloud.

"Wright brothers. You were right," Wendy says.

"Right. When the Wright brothers told everyone they were going to build a giant motorized bird and fly it through the sky . . . Were they just boys with wild imaginations?" Niimi asks.

"Or the person who invented peanut butter. Making peanuts spread like butter. Genius," Wendy adds.

Naturally, Wendy is amazed by an invention involving food.

"Or the person who invented Velcro. Talk about a time saver!" my dad says, and shows us his feet, which are encased in pinstriped Velcro slippers.

"You guys are so frustrating. Can we go now?" I grab another waffle off the plate.

"Aye. Now that we have established magic is indeed very real, we can be well on our way to start our wee adventure," Niimi says in a Scottish accent.

My dad and Wendy both widen their eyes, clearly impressed with her dialect. "Look at that—it works," Wendy says.

"Welcome to Gullible City, population, you two. Let's go," I say to them both, and walk out of the house.

Niimi meets me outside. I see one bike, with a helmet resting on the handlebars. Niimi gets on it and looks back at me. "Hop on, lad," she says.

"No way," I say. "And you can drop the accent now."

"Well, do you have your own bike?"

"No. But there's one in the garage."

"Yeah, a really nice one, but your dad says it belongs to George," she says.

"Trust me. He isn't going to use it anytime soon," I say, and head to the garage.

Niimi is halfway down the block before I catch up to her. George's bike is much nicer than hers. It still has the price tag attached to the handlebars. Wendy spent one hundred and fifty dollars on this thing, and it's just been collecting dust. I rip off the tag and toss it into the neighbor's trash can as I ride past it. I could easily get fifty bucks for this bike back home.

Niimi's fast. She whips down the street, using the wind

133

as her ally to pick up speed and drift into each turn. She looks as if she just robbed a liquor store and stole a bike to use as her getaway ride.

After thirty minutes, she finally stops in front of a small yellow wooden house. I have sweat dripping off me by the time I reach her. She hops off her bike and leans it against a white picket fence.

"You're not afraid someone will steal it if you just leave it there?" I ask.

"Of course not. The thief will be with me," she says.

I set George's bike next to hers. I'm exhausted. I had no idea I was so out of shape. I take a few deep breaths and fall into the grass, letting the sun recharge me, until she stands directly above me, blocking it.

"No time to rest. She needs us," Niimi says.

"Who needs us?"

"Her name is Lulu. This is Operation Nagamo Indigo Binesi," Niimi says.

"Nagamo Indi-what?"

"It means 'she sings like a bird.' You ready?"

"Wait. Can I ask you something before we do whatever it is we are about to do?" I ask.

"Sure."

"What does 'blooming people' even mean?"

She smiles like she was waiting for me to ask her this. "Benny, like a gardener tends to their flowers, my dad's method is to turn everyone into a beautiful rose. My method is different, more like my mother's. I help people become a different kind of rose . . . super he-rose. Get it? I make super-heroes," she says.

I laugh out loud. Her eyes shoot hot blades at me. "What's so funny about that?" she asks.

"Seriously? You don't see how that's funny?" I glance at my feet. "That's even funnier."

"Nope. I don't see the funny. Not one bit."

"First, superheroes aren't real. Those are people in comic books or movies who wear masks and capes while trying to save humankind from some poorly written villain who threatens to destroy the planet. Secondly, even if they were real, which they're not, but even if they were, super-heroes aren't made by people. You have to be a mutant from another galaxy, or be a top-secret government experiment, or be bitten by a radioactive spider like Spider-Man."

"None of those explain Batman or Iron Man."

"They're different. They're rich," I say. "But my point is, none of them are real. They're just actors playing characters pretending to do good things."

Niimi stretches her arms overhead as if she's bored by this conversation.

"Correct me if I'm wrong, Benny, but if someone pre-tends to do good, and people see their good deed and feel better about their lives from witnessing it, then go home and try to make their lives better . . . doesn't that mean the superhero did their job? Wouldn't that make it real?"

"No, because at the end of the day, the actor takes off the mask and cape and goes home to their regular life," I say.

"Like Clark Kent, Bruce Wayne, Peter Parker, Tony Stark, Steve Rogers, Logan, I mean . . . Every superhero needs a disguise, Benny. That's how it works. Thor is Thor, but when he's not saving the world, he gets to go home and pretend to be boring old Chris, an Australian dad with a six-pack and a sore back."

"That's who he really is. He's not really a superhero."

"Not to you. But to other people, he is. And today, my job is to bloom Lulu," Niimi says as she offers me her hand.

I accept it, and she lifts me up to my feet. Wow. She's a lot stronger than she looks. She hands me a pen and a note-pad. "What's this for?"

"All I need you to do is write down what I tell you to," she says.

I flip to the first page, dab the pen over my tongue to ready the ink, and look at her.

"Your body is a world. In that world there are three warriors. A superhero, someone who needs help, and a villain. But there can only be one leader of your world. My job is to wake up your superhero and help you slay the villain," she says in a deep movie-trailer voice. "That's it. Got it?"

I laugh as I jot it all down. "Got it. It's a really good bumper sticker. Kinda long, though. How about just 'If you believe in silly things like magic and superheroes, I'm your

136

girl, Chief Niimi Whatever," I say in an even deeper movie-trailer voice.

"It's not Niimi Whatever. It's Niimi Waatese . . . And I liked mine better," she says.

"Fine. But don't look at me when you get laughed at."

"I won't. And I want it memorized by nightfall. But for now, let's go wake up Lulu's superhero."

So, is this the Native boot camp? Riding bikes with a wannabe superhero maker and writing down cheesy quotes while she pretends to bloom people? This is ridiculous. But it could be worse. I could be stuck in a bookstore.

"All right. Let's go embarrass ourselves," I say, and follow her up the walkway toward the front door.

She knocks three times on the wooden door. A woman answers.

"Are you Lulu?" Niimi asks.

"Yes," she says.

Lulu is older than us. I'd say she's eighteen or nineteen. She wears a black tank top and jeans, revealing two arms covered in tattoos. Her hair is short and dyed green and black and pushed all to one side. She has a nose ring and heavy eye shadow.

"You're Niimi Waatese?" Lulu asks.

"I am, and this is my assistant, Benny," Niimi responds.

Oh great, I'm now her assistant. I went from bookstore employee to assisting a twelve-year-old girl. I think I'd prefer a boot camp with a mean drill sergeant barking orders at me all day.

"I expected your father, but if you're as good as he says you are, then I'm ready to rock and roll with you," Lulu says as she welcomes us into her home.

Inside there are boxes lining the walls, stacked and taped and ready to go. An old acoustic guitar leans against her plaid couch.

"Are you moving?" Niimi asks her.

"I've been trying to for half a year now, but I can't seem to get out the door. That's why you're here," Lulu says.

Finally, some manual labor to kick this boot camp off. She doesn't need to bloom. She just needs movers. "Want me to start carrying boxes out?" I ask.

They both look at me and smile. "Bless his heart," Lulu says.

"He's not the sharpest tooth on the jaw, but he means well," Niimi says.

"What? This is my boot camp, right? I can carry her boxes." Why they are staring at me like they just caught me trying to bite my own ears?

"How about you sit down, Benny," Niimi says.

"Whatever," I say, and lean up against the wall. "I'll stay quiet."

"Benny, please recite our mission statement to Lulu," Niimi says.

"Our what?" I ask.

Niimi points to the notepad. Oh, that thing. I don't have it memorized yet, so I flip it open and read. "Your body is a world. In that world there are three warriors. A super-hero, someone who needs help, and a villain. But there can only be one leader of your world. My job is to wake up your superhero and help you slay the villain."

I expect Lulu to laugh at what I just read, but she doesn't. Instead, she takes a deep breath and nods, as if she's processing the words. How does this punk-rocker-looking person take this seriously? Never mind the fact that Lulu looks like she'd make a pretty cool superhero, but come on, twelve-year-olds just don't show up at doorsteps handing out superpowers.

"Why don't you sit down and tell me what exactly cages your heart," Niimi says.

Lulu nods and takes a seat on the couch. Niimi pulls up a chair from the table and sets it in front of Lulu. Before she sits, she stretches her arms, legs, and torso as if she was an athlete preparing to take the field. She points to the far end of the couch, signaling me to sit . . . So I do. I get a front row seat to this circus.

A part of me feels like this is just another prank being pulled on me. A punk rock Ojibwe singer asking a twelve-year-old mask-wearing girl for help?

Come on. This is the definition of gullible.

CHAPTER 12

LULU

E ven as a young girl, music was a huge part of my life. I didn't care what was on, as long as it was playing. Classical, jazz, rap, country, punk . . . It never mattered. I grew up idolizing all the greats. So, I begged my parents for a guitar. I practiced every day. When most kids were outside playing tag, I was in my room, strumming away to Prince. When girls were out having crushes on boys, playing spin the bottle at parties, I was home, crushing on Siouxsie and Hendrix. When other teenagers turned sixteen and wanted a car, I wanted a Strat. But it didn't matter how good I got, how badly my fingers bled, or how well I could sing, because there is one thing that holds me back from my dream," she says.

"And that is?" Niimi asks.

"An absolutely crippling case of stage fright," she says.

"Prove it," Niimi says.

Lulu reaches over and picks up the guitar. She holds it like a mother holds her baby. She adjusts the strings, secures it on her lap, and takes a deep breath. *STRUM.*

The melody is beautiful. And she knows it. It's catchy. But the expression on Lulu's face completely kills the vibe. She looks scared. She wants to sing, but she doesn't. Her mouth opens on every break, but no words come out. She just looks like a deer staring at an oncoming truck. She stops playing. "It's always the same," she says as she sets the guitar down.

"What are you afraid of?" Niimi asks.

"I don't know."

"Have you tried—"

"I've tried everything. I tried closing my eyes, I tried turning around with my back to everyone, I even pictured everyone naked. Nothing works."

Niimi scratches her chin, thinking . . .

"How do we know you just don't suck?" I ask.

Niimi and Lulu glare at me like I suggested drowning a kitten.

"I'm serious. Maybe she shreds the guitar, but can't sing?"

Lulu hisses, "I can sing!"

"Forgive my assistant, Lulu. He has a hole in his heart," Niimi says.

"I do not. I am asking a valid question," I add.

"Follow me. I'll show you how good I am," Lulu says, and leads us to the back bedroom.

Her bedroom has been transformed into a small recording studio. There is a mic stand, a couple guitars against the walls, and a desk. Atop the desk is an open laptop and synthesizer. The walls are covered in egg cartons, stapled from floor to ceiling, completely encasing the room.

"Wow. That's a lot of eggs," Niimi says.

Lulu laughs. "It soundproofs the room."

"Having all this stuff still doesn't prove you can sing," I say.

Lulu walks over to her laptop and mashes a few keys and flips the volume up. A buzz hums across the room from the large speakers placed in each corner.

"But this does," she says, and hits one last key. A guitar melody fills the room. "This is me," Lulu says.

Lulu directs the laptop screen to face us.

Dressed in a black gothic dress, fashionably torn and hugging her body, she stares into the camera and sings . . . Lulu's voice floats out of the speakers, beautifully, like a butterfly fluttering off a flower.

> I've been dreamin' of a dragon
> Draggin' me down, underground
> To its lair.
> But I didn't care
> I thought I deserved it

I thought I was worthless
But I was wrong.
So I wrote this song
And now care, I do
Because I am anew
A new Lulu
And tonight, I'll fight back
And tonight, I'll bite back
I'll slay the dragon, I'll slay my dragon
My song of fire—

Lulu closes her laptop, abruptly ending the song.

She stares at me with a cocky smirk. "So, you still think I suck?" Lulu asks.

Niimi claps. "No. You're the opposite of suck. I mean, I don't condone slaying dragons or any animals for that matter, but Lulu, you are the perfect medicine for struggling ears."

"What does your assistant think?" Lulu asks, and they both look at me as if I were a judge letting her know if she made it to the next round of a talent competition.

"Honestly . . . I think . . . you're amazing," I add. "In a real fight, I think a dragon would defeat you easily, but for a song, it was really good. It definitely belongs on the radio."

"Right?" Lulu smiles. "And this song has a million views. I have two other videos with double that. And next week I'm supposed to perform at the North House Folk

School in front of a room full of music executives flying in from Nashville. I've packed my entire life in boxes to move to the Twin Cities. My career is out there, just waiting for me, but I can't . . . As hard as I try . . . If there's a crowd, my birds won't fly," she says.

Niimi approaches her and circles like a vulture. Lulu shifts uncomfortably in her chair, "What are you doing?" Lulu asks.

"Thinking. Tell me, Lulu . . . When did you first discover this fear?"

"I used to perform for my parents when I was your age. I loved the attention. Imagine that. They'd watch me for hours. I'd change outfits and lip sync to Red Hot Chili Peppers, Dolly Parton, Radiohead, Sheryl Crow . . . I knew every song by heart. My mom and dad even helped me with my hair and makeup. Everything was in its right place . . . But then . . . at my eighth-grade talent show, the day after my parents separated, I was going to perform a Lady Gaga song, but . . . I just stood there. I couldn't sing. I was Lady Nada. Nothing came out. And it's been like that ever since."

"But if you're alone?" Niimi asks.

"If I'm alone, I can sing to the moon and back."

"Interesting . . . My assistant and I are going to head back to our office and—"

"We don't have an office," I add.

"Correction. My assistant and I are going to take a walk and come up with a game plan. We'll be back shortly."

"So, you think you can fix me?" Lulu asks.

"There's nothing to fix, because you are not broken. There's just a villain inside you, and that villain conquered your mind and kicked you offstage. Your songs are held captive somewhere near your throat. But the superhero inside of you is in there too. We just need to wake her up and let them fight it out. That's the only way for your voice to be free," Niimi says.

I stifle my laughter. Who does this girl think she is?

"Miigwech," Lulu says, her voice soft with relief. "Your mother bloomed my uncle a few years ago. If you're even half as gifted as she was, then I'm in good hands."

Lulu and Niimi walk out of the room. "You coming?" Niimi asks.

"Yeah, I just wanna write that down. I'll be right there," I say.

Once I hear them talking in the front of the house, I turn to the microphone case behind Lulu's desk. This looks expensive. I could get some serious cash for it. My blood begins to rush. It's the familiar adrenaline coursing through me. The need to take something that isn't mine. The need to prove I can. To show this boot camp, whenever it starts, that I can do whatever I want, including taking whatever I want, whenever I want, from whoever I want. I open my backpack and stuff a shiny black microphone inside.

Lulu walks us to the front door and hugs Niimi goodbye. She offers me a handshake. I'm not sure if she likes me or not, but to be fair, I don't think making new friends is a high priority for her. Or me. She just wants to sing. I just want to get this over with.

Niimi passes our bikes and continues down the street. I rush over to join her.

She turns off the sidewalk path and heads into the forest. I stop.

"Aren't there wild animals in there?"

"Don't be scared. I'll protect you."

"How? I'm bigger than you."

"Yeah. But I'm smarter."

Okay. I guess when she's trying to outsmart the wolf, that will buy me enough time to run. So I hurry to keep up with her.

CHAPTER 13

MADWEWECHIGE (SHE PLAYS MUSIC)

I hear birds chirping, but I can't see them, and it makes me uneasy. Like I'm being watched but can't see the watcher. I guess that's how nature is: always curious, always there. I've never really been around nature before. Duluth has parks, but I stuck to shopping places like Matterhorn, Miller Hill Mall, and Stoneridge; after all, there's nothing to steal in a forest.

As we venture deeper in, I keep wondering why Lulu didn't say anything about Niimi's appearance. I guess everyone around here knows about Niimi and her mask? Everyone but me.

Niimi stops. "What do you see?" she asks me.

"What do you mean? I see trees."

"Exactly," she says, and keeps walking.

Huh? Was that supposed to mean something? "What are we doing out here?" I ask.

"Searching for answers."

"We aren't gonna find out why Lulu has stage fright by getting lost in the woods," I say as I pick my way over branches and rocks.

"If we get lost, we'll need to be found. So, by that same logic, if the answers are also lost, we just need to find them. Or they need to find us. They're here. I can feel them. Now, stop the jaw-joggin' and help me look," she says.

This girl. I can't figure her out. "What exactly am I looking for?"

"Well, answers are usually right in front of you, so look there, but they also tend to be where you least expect them to be, so look there too," she says.

"I least expect them to be in this forest," I say.

"Exactly," she says, and gets on all fours, clawing at the dirt and shoving twigs this way and that way.

I want to laugh, but I also want to get this over with so we can return to civilization.

"Okay. What exactly do answers look like?" I ask.

"They are tricky little things. Sometimes they disguise themselves as questions. And sometimes they hide in fear, like how hermit crabs hide in shells."

"How will I know if I find it? Does fear bite? Is fear dangerous?"

"My daddy says if you see fear, confront it. Fear is usually afraid of confrontation. Remember, fear's more afraid of you than you are afraid of it."

"So, you're not afraid of fear?" This conversation is going in circles. "Isn't fear supposed to be . . . feared?"

"No, Benny. I'm not afraid of anything."

"Impossible," I say. "Everyone's afraid of something."

"I've seen a lot of scary things in my life. I know fear very well. And I also know its weakness." She whispers into my ear, "Fear is afraid of you not giving in to it. If you don't, it loses its power over you. And without its power, there's nothing to fear about fear. It will eventually give up on you and go find someone else to scare the crap out of."

"I don't buy it. What about spiders?" I ask.

Niimi laughs. "Totally misunderstood creatures. Plus, I happen to speak Arachnid. I'm not fluent, but I understand enough to know that they are good eight-legged peoples," she says. "If people understood them more, they'd actually love spiders. They're perfect roommates. They make your home a no-fly zone."

It's not like I've been taking notes, but this is maybe the most ridiculous thing she has said so far. I immediately scan my surroundings for a hidden camera that is documenting this elaborate prank on me . . . But it's just us. I am literally wandering around the forest with a girl who thinks she can outsmart wolves and speak to spiders.

"You're not afraid of dying?" I ask.

"Death is just a staircase, and I'm not afraid of heights," she snaps back.

"I'm starting to see that your mask is the least odd thing about you," I say.

"Good. You're still learning."

I'm guessing she'll just wiggle her way out of every scenario if I keep this line of questioning up. I may as well start looking for fear. I get down on my knees and mimic her. After sifting through the dirt for a minute or so, Niimi shouts, "Eya!"

I know that one. That means yes. I get up and walk to her. She lies on the ground, ear to the earth. "I'm afraid to ask, but . . . what are you doing now?"

"I hear the answer. It's saying something," she says.

"No, you don't. You're just pressing your ear to the dirty ground. What you hear is probably insects," I say.

"Listen for yourself." She pats the ground beside her.

I sigh and lower my body to the ground, placing my ear in the dirt. I hear nothing.

"Listen carefully," Niimi whispers. "Not with your ears, but with your brain. Ears are just outlets. You need to connect to the vibrations of the aki."

I listen, and as soon as I'm about to tell her how useless this is, I actually hear something. A hum. A light hum under the dirt. Almost like a distant approaching train. What is that?

"You hear it, don't you?" she says.

"I hear something. But I don't know what it is," I say.

"That's the answer. Lucky for you, I also understand Earth-tongue."

"Yeah. That's not a thing," I say.

"Of course it's a thing. It's everything. We all understand it," she says.

"We?"

"The animals, the trees, the wind and water, all the rocks and dirt. It's just us humans who have forgotten how to communicate with the earth," she says. "Before we had cars and buildings and desk jobs and bank accounts, all of this was common sense. It came to us naturally. Nature speaks to whoever will listen. And I am listening."

"So the answer is in the ground?" I ask.

"It sees us. But . . . Maybe it's not staring up at us. Maybe it's staring down at us. Lie on your back and stare up at it," she says, flipping her body over and staring straight up to the sky.

I do the same, and for a few moments, we lie perfectly still. We probably look like two dead bodies left in the forest by some serial killer.

"Now what do you see?" she asks.

"I see trees, the sky, maybe a cloud—that's it," I say.

"So, you see it too," she says happily.

"See what?" I ask.

"An audience." She sits up. "There's our answer."

I stare up, and I guess, in a way, I kind of see what she

means. The tall trees, the sky, the passing cloud do resemble an audience. And they are all around us, staring at us—well, they would be if they had eyes.

"Even if these trees look like an audience, how does that help Lulu?" I ask.

"Lulu has stage fright because she can't perform in front of people. I believe her brain convinced her to stop singing because her parents split up. She sees everyone as her mom and dad. And her voice couldn't keep them together. So it stopped working. That leaves only two solutions for us. One, we get her parents back together, which is not going to happen, I know them. So that leaves us with only one way to save Lulu."

"And that is what?" I ask.

"We convince her that she's never been alone, even when she thought she was."

"I'm not following," I say.

"Think about it. The trees, rocks, birds, bugs, and whatever else is in here watching us, are alive too. We are not alone. We need her to know that she's been performing in front of living things this entire time. Her dresser, her guitar, her walls, they all come from wood. That means they were once trees, like these ones here. Her couch spends many hours a day with her. Her bed cradles her in its arms when she dreams. Her clothes hold and hug her all day and night. Comforting her, supporting her. She's never alone. Lulu needs to see that. Come on, we have a lot of work to do," Niimi says, and walks back the way we came.

"Wait! Her bed cradles her? Her clothes hug her? Her walls are trees? Do you hear yourself? None of what you just said makes sense."

"Sense, sense, sense. You want everything to always make sense."

"Yeah. If it doesn't make sense, it's called nonsense. Like everything you just said."

"Benny, when we enter this world, we are given six senses. Sight. You see it, you believe it. Smell, you smell it, you believe it. Taste, you taste it, you believe it. Hearing, you hear it, you believe it. Touch, you touch it, you believe it."

"That's five. We have five senses."

"Sense number six. Feel. You feel it, you believe it. And I feel it. You've just convinced yourself that your sixth sense doesn't work. You forgot how to feel. That's why none of this makes sense to you. Don't use your eyes, ears, tongue, hands, or nose. Feel it in your heart."

Where does she come up with this bumper sticker stuff? And she's wrong. I didn't forget how to feel. In fact, I feel like I want to get out of this darn forest! I feel very strongly about that.

I follow her out of the forest, and when we reach Lulu's home, near our bikes, Lulu is pacing back and forth on the lawn, waiting for us.

"Did you come up with a plan?" Lulu asks.

"Yes," Niimi says. "But in order for it to work quickly and efficiently in time for your upcoming performance, I will need some money for a few much-needed supplies."

"How much?" Lulu asks.

"I don't know, maybe one hundred dollars," Niimi replies.

Lulu digs into her pocket and pulls out some cash. She counts it. "I have sixty. I don't get paid for another two weeks," she says.

"Sixty will do. It will just force me to be a bit more creative, which is always a challenge I will eagerly accept. In fact, we'll make it an even fifty," Niimi says, and accepts the money from Lulu.

"Wait. You're paying this girl fifty dollars to solve your stage fright? That doesn't seem ridiculous to you? I mean, I steal from people, but this is highway robbery," I say, finding this all to be a bit too unbelievable.

"What my assistant fails to understand is that every problem has a solution. He is of the mindset that you're required to play the hand you're dealt, not realizing that all this time, you've held the entire deck of cards. You don't like your hand, shuffle again. Lulu, I promise you that you and I will not stop shuffling your deck until you're satisfied with the cards in front of you."

"Did you read that on a bumper sticker too?" I ask.

"No. It's something my mom told me," she says, and I

immediately shut up because I remember what I said last night about her mom. Ugh. I asked her dad if he laughed when his wife died. I do not want to remind her of that. I should have never said it.

"I trust you. I don't trust him, though," Lulu says, pointing to me. "I actually feel sorry for him."

"Don't feel sorry for me," I snap. "I'm not the one who just threw fifty bucks away."

"We'll see," Lulu says, and turns to Niimi, "So what do I do now?"

"Practice. We'll be back later with the necessities."

Before Lulu goes back inside, Niimi leans in and whispers something into her ear. I'm too far away to hear it, but Lulu looks at me and nods.

I bet she's telling Lulu not to take anything I say personally. Or maybe she's telling her that this is all a big prank and she's thanking her for playing along. I am starting to believe there is no boot camp. I think I'm just babysitting Niimi while she goes out and plays in the forest pretending to talk to spiders and dirt.

"What did you say to her?" I ask.

"You'll *knows* soon enough," Niimi says.

"I'll *knows* soon enough?"

Niimi smiles and hands me the money before she gets onto her bike.

"What do you want me to do with all of this?" I ask.

"I have another person to bloom, so we're going to have

to split up for a few hours. What I need you to do is wait five minutes, knock on Lulu's door, and convince her to go shopping with you. With the money, you will purchase as many stuffed animals as you can possibly carry. But the most important part is to make sure that Lulu sings every sentence she speaks, to you or anyone else you come into contact with, understand?"

"Are you kidding?" I say, and shake my head. "I'm not doing any of that."

"Oh, yes you are, Benny, and I'll tell you why. Because if you don't, I'll inform your dad that you are uncooperative. He will have no choice but to send you back, and he will then relay our disappointment to your mother, who will undoubtedly hand you back over to the handsome judge," Niimi says as she puts on her helmet and begins to ride away.

"He wasn't even that handsome," I shout. "And what kind of boot camp is this, anyway?"

Boot camps are supposed to be filled with manual labor, aren't they? Shouldn't there be a thick-skinned dude with a buzz cut and a cigar hanging out of his mouth trying to whip me into shape by making me do push-ups and having me scale walls? Why am I not being yelled at? Why is there no one telling me how worthless I am?

And how does Niimi know so much about what's going on with me? How does she know about my mom? The judge? Is she trying to prove to me that she can "bloom" me by showing me she can help Lulu?

156

Well, I got news for her. I don't bloom. Or maybe . . . this is a test to see if I'll steal the money. I've already thought about it. I should take it. I should ride back home and not worry about some girl's stage fright. Lulu needs to grow up and face the music, literally.

But . . . it would be so ironic if what got me here is a ridiculous stuffed animal and what sends me back is refusing to buy fifty bucks' worth of more ridiculous stuffed animals.

The words *final chance* ring in my head. Maybe I should just do it. Lulu will be the one looking like a fool, singing to everyone she encounters. I'll just step back and deny I'm with her.

I walk up to Lulu's door and knock three times.

She doesn't answer. Oh, well, I tried. Not my fault if she doesn't open her door. I take my first step off the porch, and the front door swings open. I turn around and see Lulu stepping out of her house and approaching me.

I start to explain the plan. "So, I'm now supposed to go with you to—"

CRACK!

Before I can finish my sentence, Lulu swings and her fist slams straight into my nose. I stumble back, tripping over my own feet, and hit the ground.

Pain sears into my brain. My eyes immediately well up and leak. It feels like hot steam is releasing through my nostrils. I taste blood. An alarm sounds off in my head screaming, "Damage!" I look up; my vision is shook. I see two Lulus. I try to blink it out as the two of her merge into one angry Lulu. "What was that for?"

"Before Niimi left, she whispered for me to check my room to see if anything was missing," Lulu says. "And guess what?"

I reach into my backpack and pull out her microphone. Ugh. Why do all people have that same look of betrayal on their face whenever I steal something of theirs? We're not friends. And people steal. That's how the world works. Get over it. I hand it back to her.

"This was a gift from someone very special to me. You touch it again, and I will bury you in this yard. We clear?" she says.

"Sorry," I say.

Now Niimi's words make sense. I'll knows soon enough. I'll nose soon enough. Yeah, my nose now knows.

I'm starting to think that maybe hightailing it out of here with the fifty bucks in my pocket was the better choice.

"Hello? What do you want?" Lulu says.

I snap out of my daze, realizing I'm still standing on her porch. I must have zoned out and imagined it as I was waiting for her to answer her door. What was that? A daydream? It felt so real. I rub my nose for confirmation. It's perfectly fine. That was so . . .

"Hello?" she says again. "Is there a reason you're standing on my porch?"

"Oh yeah. Sorry. I'm supposed to take you shopping to get the supplies for your blooming or whatever," I say.

Lulu laughs. "How's that going to look, me hanging out with a kid?" she says.

"It will look sketchy, especially if you punch me again," I say.

She looks confused. "When did I punch you?"

"You didn't. But please don't."

"All right. Just keep your hands to yourself, and you won't get punched."

"Fair enough. So . . . you got a bike?" I ask.

She smiles. "I don't have a bike, but I do have a dragon," she says, and points out to the street.

I turn to see it: a motorcycle straight out of Mad Max parked on the curb. If this girl wasn't a badass rock star a minute ago, she most definitely is now. I step off the porch and approach it. And sure enough, *Lulu's Dragon* is written across its body.

"You think you can keep up with her?" Lulu asks.

I look at George's bike. If her ride is a dragon, this bike is just a lizard. "Definitely not."

"Then hold on tight," she says, and dangles a set of keys in her hand.

Looks like I'm about to die.

CHAPTER 14

DRAGON BREATH

As we rip through the open roads, I hold on to Lulu for dear life and keep thinking about that weird blip in time where she punched me for stealing her microphone. Is this what *guilt* feels like? She doesn't even know I took it, and if she finds out, it will be so long from now and I'll hopefully be long gone.

I'm free; I should feel like it.

We enter the MN-61 S highway, and her dragon roars as we weave through traffic, like we're flying through the sky, dodging metal car clouds. Every other car we pass honks, and drivers shake their fists at us. Half the time my eyes are sealed shut, but Lulu is acting like this is as natural as breathing for her; every near collision is met with a laugh from her. I feel her chuckling as I nearly pee my pants. On one side of us is the Sun Blue Lake Superior; on the other side are green and orange trees whipping past my eyes as we pick up speed.

Thirty minutes later, I hop off as soon as she parks in the parking lot. The sign says we are at the Lake Superior Trading Post. As I take a step, my legs still feel like they're vibrating. "First time on a dragon?" she asks.

"I've never even ridden a horse," I say.

"What? Now, that's just sad."

"But I do know places like this like the back of my hand," I say, and point toward the multilevel shopping center.

"And you're proud of that?" she asks.

"Yeah. Usually my friends and I spend the first hour sweeping the lot," I say.

"What's that mean?" Lulu asks.

"We search for expensive cars, and after we choose a few, we check the doors. You'd be surprised how many people don't lock their doors. After we take whatever we can, we stash the stuff behind a dumpster, then we hit the mall," I say.

"You sound like you're not ashamed of anything you just told me," she says.

"I just want you to know that I'm really good at something," I say.

"Being good at something bad shouldn't make you feel good. It just makes you a jerk, really. It's lazy. It's boring. Now, if you really want everyone to swoon when they see you, try being a bad boy but still being a good person. Real bad boys are kind. And being kind . . . now, that's hot."

"Be a bad boy but a good person? I'm confused," I say.

"You're young. You have time to figure it all out."

"So, do you like good person bad boys?"

"I rock the niizh manidoowag flag," she says.

"The what?" I ask.

"You know, I dance to the two spirit beat," she clarifies.

"I don't understand anything you're saying."

She laughs. "I play for the other team," she says, and sends me a wink.

"What does that even . . . Oh, you mean you, like, good person bad girls?"

"You're quick. Now, let's go shopping, shall we?" she says, and starts to walk toward the shopping center.

"Wait!" I shout. "There's one rule that Niimi gave. I'm just letting you know what it is in case she asks you about it, but you don't have to do it. I'll pretend you did. It'll be our little secret," I say.

She looks intrigued. "What exactly is this rule?"

"Everyone you interact with, instead of speaking to them, you have to sing your sentences to them," I say.

Lulu laughs. "Are you serious? Did you forget the whole reason why you are here is because I can't perform in front of people?"

"Now you see why I found you paying her fifty dollars was so funny?" I say.

"Yeah. But I already forked over the money so you better think of something."

"Me? My job is to just . . . I don't know what my job is. I honestly have no idea what I'm doing here. I'm supposed to be scrubbing toilets and washing cars or something. I have no idea how to make you sing. I'm just a thief."

"A thief steals, so freaking steal my stage fright away."

I laugh, but then a thought bounces around in my brain. I'm good at stealing and she's good at singing. But in order to be a good thief, I have to get into character. I always play a browsing customer. Maybe Lulu can use this method too. Maybe she just needs to get into character. "Whenever I steal, I don't enter the store as a thief. I walk in just like everyone else; as a customer," I say.

"What's your point?"

"My point is, Lulu is afraid to sing, right? So, don't be Lulu in there. Just be a boring customer they'll never see again. That way, when you sing to them, it won't be you. Lulu the punk rock girl can wait out here, on her dragon."

Lulu considers my idea . . . "You think that will work?"

"Beats me, but if I just blew fifty bucks on a pair of shoes, I'd make sure as hell I'd be wearing them until they fell off."

"Meaning?" she asks.

"Meaning, use up every penny you just spent. It's probably a stupid idea, but give it a shot. If Cookoo can't sing either, then you're back to being Lulu who can't sing."

"Cookoo? That's my character's name? Ha. I love it. Let's see if it works. Now . . . what are we shopping for, exactly?"

"Stuffed animals," I say and walk on.

We enter the shopping center, which would usually remind me of home. But this mall is different. I wouldn't even call it a mall. I thought no matter where you are, all malls look and smell exactly the same. They're always the color of a dentist's office and smell like you just got sprayed by a perfume skunk. And they always play the same annoying holiday music that won't leave your head for days. But this place is all wooden inside, and the shops all look like friendly little mom and pop spots. It reminds me of the Old West, even though I'm not old and I've never been out west.

As Lulu and I pass the various stores, my eyes wander in, picking out things to steal whenever I have the chance to come here alone. It would be easier here, there are fewer people in this trading post. Fewer people means fewer employees. Fewer employees means fewer eyes on me.

"There's the toy store," she says, and heads in.

We pass the aisle of action figures, dolls, puzzles, and board games, heading straight to the clearance section near the back. The area is topped floor to ceiling with discounted stuffed animals. "Which ones do we get?" Lulu sings to me.

"I really don't think it matters," I say, holding back a laugh.

"Awesome," Lulu sings, and pulls down a possum. "Take as many as you can carry."

I pull down an otter, a wolf, a loon, a moose, a bunny, and a deer. Lulu fills her arms with a horse, a monkey, a lion, a great white shark, and a giant turtle. When we can't carry any more, we approach the register, where an older woman with neon pink lipstick greets us.

"You guys building an ark in the backyard?" the woman asks with a smile.

"Oh, no. We're just—"

"Sing it!" I interrupt Lulu.

She stares at me and nods. After a beat, she begins to sing. "No, friendly lady, we're just . . . Ahh . . . I can't do it."

"Fine. Don't worry. I'll still say you did," I assure her.

"No! I'm done being quiet," Lulu says, and closes her eyes.

"Need a minute?" the woman asks, completely confused by what's going on.

I stare at Lulu. "Cookoo? You in there?"

Her eyes slowly open. She inhales a deep breath. "All of these animals, we'd like to purchase, and before you ask, yes, I'm singing on purpose. And to answer your question, we're not building an ark, because if we were, why would I need this shark?" Lulu sings to the lady.

Wow. I'm impressed. Lulu rocked it.

The cashier lady looks as if she's on the verge of laughing but doesn't, because maybe the situation is just a bit too

165

strange to be funny. "Okay, then. I'll just start singing—I mean, ringing you up," she says, and lets out a giggle while she scans the animals' tags.

This lady is funny. I bet she's an awesome grandma to some lucky kid.

"Thank you so much, and here's the money," Lulu sings, and hands the woman the cash. Then she picks up one of the stuffed animals that fell on the floor and hands it to her. "Don't forget the bunny."

The woman scans the final animal. "Forty-two dollars."

"Looks like we have enough money for at least one more. Go pick the last one and meet me at the front of the store," Lulu sings to me.

I make my way back to the wall of stuffed animals. I just need one. It doesn't matter which one, so I reach for the closest. But . . . I freeze.

The animal my hand lands on is none other than the bear. The same exact stuffed bear that got me into this whole mess. The same exact stuffed bear that gave me this same exact frozen feeling the last time I saw it. Back in Duluth it was twenty bucks. Here it's on sale for four bucks. I don't care if it's free, I still don't want it.

"Not you again."

I stand there, completely still, wondering why I can't move. What is it about this stuffed bear that glues me to the floor? I need to breathe. I exhale and hear the shallowness in the escaping air. I'm scared, but I don't know why. I'm not even sure if it's fear. Maybe it's sadness? Maybe it's anxiety? Nerves? I don't know; they all feel the same right now. I look into its glassy black plastic eyes and hope to see the answer, but I see nothing resembling one . . . Just a stuffed bear staring back at me, its gaze frozen, like mine.

"Jeez, Mr. Indecisive, I said I don't care," Lulu sings from behind me. "Let's just take this bear."

She shoves me aside, grabs the bear by its left paw, and carries it to the register.

I want to scream, *No! Not that one! Any one but that one!* But my voice isn't working yet. I try to breathe slowly until my body finally unthaws and returns to normal. And by the time it does, it's too late. Lulu has bought the bear and left the store.

What just happened? I run to catch up with her. My legs feel like jellyfish. Lulu, however, has a newfound pep in her step. I should offer to carry the humongous bag she's carrying, but that freaking bear is in there. "You okay?" she asks, sensing my nerves.

"Yeah. I just need to pee. I'll meet you back at your dragon," I say, and rush off deeper into the shopping center.

But I don't need to pee. Instead, I need to feel normal again. I need to feel like me. And I know exactly what that means. I need to steal something.

I dip into the nearest store, which happens to be a clothing store. That's good. Clothes are easy to shoplift. As I enter, I focus on my five rules. I need to be smart and professional this time. No getting caught. No mistakes. I approach a round glass display table filled with shirts on hangers. I pluck four but remove a fifth one from the hanger and stuff it between the other four and walk up to the guy near the fitting room.

"I'd like to try these on," I say to him.

He counts my hangers and hands me a bendable tag with a number four on it. "Just hang this outside the fitting room door," he says, and walks me to the changing room.

"You from Grand Marais, or you just visiting?" the man asks through the door.

Why do people in small towns always want to chat? It's so annoying that people feel the need to be friendly to faces they've never seen before. I'm here to steal. That's it.

"Umm. Just visiting," I shout back.

"Whereabouts from?" he replies.

Ugh. Old man, leave me alone. We are not friends. I need to think of somewhere that will shut him up . . . "Hawaii. And I'm really jet-lagged. Too tired to talk," I shout back.

Technically, I'm not lying. I was standing in Hawaii earlier today.

It worked. I hear his feet shuffle away as he shouts, "If you got time, you should swing by the Lighthouse. It was lit in 1922 and is still operational today. Ain't that something?"

"I'll check it out. Thanks," I shout back, knowing I won't do any such thing.

Finally, alone inside, I pick the shirt that I'd most likely wear. After all, if I'm going to steal it, I may as well like it. Let's see what we got here . . . My choices are a white shirt with a hangman on it. It reads HOW'S IT HANGIN'? . . . No thanks. Too cheesy.

The second shirt is a blue shirt that has a picture of a small can of pop on it, that stands on a doormat. And on it is WELCOME TO MINI SODA . . . Umm, nope. Even cheesier.

The third shirt is red and has a drawing of a moose on it. The moose is covered in chocolate. Under the moose it says CHOCOLATE MOOSE. Maybe I'll come back later and steal this shirt for Wendy. She loves food. She loves eating so much that she'd probably eat a moose.

The next shirt is black and has a picture of a dragon on it, breathing fire, but the fire is a blue frost-flame, and the dragon is holding breath mints. Under it, it says DRAGON BREATH. I don't really get it, but Lulu will. I found a winner.

I take a quick glance at the last shirt, which is gray and says OUR LAKE IS SUPERIOR and has a picture of Lake Superior during sunset. I immediately think my mom would like this shirt, which makes me feel kind of guilty for not talking to her yet. She probably misses me like crazy. Maybe later I'll get this shirt for her. But not right now; I'm not here to feel, I'm here to steal.

I remove my shirt, put on the dragon shirt, and slip my shirt back on over it. I then put all four shirts back on the four hangers and open the door. The guy takes the shirts from me.

"How'd you do, buddy?" he asks.

"None fit right," I say, and exit the store. "But I'll be back."

"Aloha," he says as I walk toward the front entrance.

Aloha? Oh, that's right. I'm supposed to be Hawaiian. "Aloha," I say back.

I feel better. I feel like myself again. I walk outside and see Lulu, who is on her motorcycle, waiting for me by the curb. "That was quite the bathroom break, kid, what's the matter with your bladder?" she sings to me, and tosses me the helmet.

"You can stop singing now," I say, which causes her to laugh.

I slap on the helmet, and we race out of the parking lot and onto Wisconsin Street, so fast that I almost pee my pants again, which would take some explaining, since she thinks I just peed.

Within thirty minutes we are back at her home. I bet an average driver takes much longer to get back to Grand Portage, but the average driver doesn't ride a dragon. And as we pull up to her house, I can't believe it, but George's brandnew bike is still exactly where I left it. People up here are so trusting. Don't they realize there are thieves around? Lulu parks her dragon on the curb and grabs the bag of stuffed animals from one of the dragon's compartments. I remove the helmet and climb off, following her.

She stops at the door. "So . . . what am I supposed to do with all these animals?" she asks.

"Beats me."

"Okay, well, until Niimi comes back, I'm going to get some work done," she says.

"Meaning I should leave?" I ask.

"Meaning exactly that."

I hold the screen door open for her. "Can I ask you something?"

"I just always have been," she says.

"What?" I ask.

"Were you not going to ask me what everyone else asks me when they find out I'm gay?" she says.

"No. I was going to ask you if you knew why Niimi wears that mask," I say.

Lulu smiles, though I'm not sure why. "You got the hots for her, don't you?"

"What? No!"

Plus, it's impossible to have the hots for someone in a place so cold.

"Have you asked Niimi?" she says.

"Ask me what?" Niimi says from behind me, approaching the porch.

I turn and try to recover, hoping she didn't overhear me. "Hey. We were just talking about what we should do with all these animals," I say.

"Was he asking why I wear this mask?" Niimi asks Lulu.

"Yep."

"And did you tell him about the leaking radioactive

plant that is directly behind my house that has turned the upper half of my face into red blistering bubbles?" Niimi says.

"I didn't get to that, but I was going to, right after the one about you being bit in the forehead by a great white Lake Superior shark," Lulu says.

Niimi and Lulu laugh.

"It's a valid question. Normal people don't wear masks," I say.

"Normal people?" Niimi looks around. "Have you seen a normal person around here, Lulu?"

"I haven't seen a normal person around here in ages. In fact, I don't even remember what they look like. Tell us, Benny, what does a normal person look like?" Lulu asks.

"Well . . . like me," I say, and they both erupt in laughter.

"You're a riot, Benny. But the time for hahas is over. Let's go inside and root out this fear," Niimi says, and passes me as she enters Lulu's home. I follow them in.

Once inside, Niimi empties the bag of stuffed animals onto the carpeted floor.

I turn away so I don't have to see the stuffed bear again.

"Benny, move this couch and coffee table to the back wall," Niimi says, and since there is no point in refusing, I do it.

"Lulu, do you have chairs?"

"In the kitchen, and some foldouts in the garage," Lulu says.

"Great. Get those," Niimi says.

"Okay, umm, why?" Lulu asks as she heads into the kitchen.

"For your concert. Hurry up. Your show starts in five minutes."

I move the couch and coffee table. Lulu brings in four table chairs and five foldout chairs. Niimi sets them up in rows; a first and second row, then places the stuffed animals into each chair, facing the front; where Lulu will be performing. The remaining stuffed animals are placed on the couch, making it the back row. The cheap seats. I keep my eyes on Lulu. I do not want to freeze up again by staring at the bear.

"Hit the lights," Niimi says to me even though she's much closer to the switch than I am, but again, I do it; strictly out of curiosity.

Niimi hands Lulu the guitar and nudges her to the front and center of the room, as if her living room is a stage. Lulu takes a deep breath. She looks hesitant.

"They're just stuffed animals. Don't worry," Niimi says.

"But you two are watching. You're not animals," Lulu responds.

"Technically, we are animals, but would it help you if we blended into the crowd?" Niimi asks.

Lulu looks confused, "How can you blend into this crowd?"

Niimi smiles and reaches into her bag, pulling out two

173

life-size animal costumes; one brown and orange turkey and one pink pig. "You want to be the mizise or the gookoosh?" she asks.

I really need to learn Ojibwe. "I'll be the turkey."

"Put it on," Niimi says as she tosses the gobbler to me.

"Where do you conjure up these ideas?" I ask Niimi.

"Conjure. Good word. Write that down."

"I just said it. It's my word. Why would I write it down?" I ask.

"It's my notebook. And my pen. Write it down."

I write it down and take the turkey-wear with me to Lulu's bathroom. After I shut the door, I remove my shirt, and my new shirt, and unzip the turkey costume. I shuffle it over my jeans and zip it up. My reflection makes me laugh. I look even sillier than when my dad and Wendy dressed me up in that ninety-nine cent Indian costume.

As soon as I waddle into the living room, I am greeted by Niimi, dressed as a pig with a mask. I toss Lulu the dragon breath shirt and take a seat. Lulu catches it and downs her eyebrows at me. "Where did you get this?" she asks me.

"It's mine, but I think it suits you better. You can have it," I say.

"It's new?"

"Nah, I've had it for ages," I say.

"But it still has the price tag on it," she says, holding it up for me to see.

Niimi shoots me a look of disappointment. "We'll deal with this later, Benny," Niimi says.

Lulu removes her top. She wears a red bra, and her skin is adorned with more tattoos. This girl must enjoy pain. She puts on her new shirt. It fits tightly over her body, and she immediately bites the seam lines of the sleeves, then rips them off, making it sleeveless. "That's better," she says.

"You just bit the sleeves off the shirt. Who does that?" I say.

"Dragons do," Lulu says.

Lulu begins to strum her guitar. The crowd of stuffed animals is her audience. This is pretty ridiculous. But let's see if Niimi's plan works. I guess we'll soon find out if Lulu just flushed fifty dollars down the toilet.

CHAPTER 15

GASHKENDAMIDE'E (SAD HEART)

I call this song 'Bring It On,'" Lulu says, and continues to strum her guitar.

> *If today doesn't kill me, tomorrow might.*
> *But I won't go easily—just ask last night.*
> *Yes, I slayed yesterday, and I defeated the day before.*
> *When I got knocked down, I got back up and asked for more.*
> *I massacred Monday, I tore apart Tuesday*
> *I buried Wednesday with Thursday*
> *I finished Friday, and drowned the weekend in the creek*
> *And all of that was just last week.*
> *Right now is upon me, the past is dead and gone*
> *And I'm staring at my future, singing "Bring it on" . . .*

As Lulu sings, my eyes start playing tricks on me. Maybe because the room is dimly lit and there's so much nervous energy, but I keep thinking I see the stuffed animals begin to move. I know it's impossible, but from the corners of my eyes I see an ear twitch, then an arm move. But as soon as I shoot my eyes to each animal, they stop moving. And then moments later, it happens again. A tail wags, a head nods. But every time I try to catch them in the act, they go still again. It's always in my peripheral vision. Maybe I'm just tired or hungry or something. But I notice Lulu's eyes widen, and she nearly gasps every time her eyes meet her audience. Are we both seeing this?

Lulu stops playing and sets the guitar down. Hands shaking. Niimi and I, and all the stuffed animals, sit in silence as we watch Lulu cry. After a few beats, Niimi stands up and claps. I do the same, half expecting the stuffed animals to join the standing ovation, but they don't move. Lulu smiles and wipes away her tears.

"Your superhero is waking up," Niimi says.

Lulu can barely speak. "How did I . . . I mean, how did you . . ."

"It's simple," Niimi says. "I realized to look forward, we must look back. The Anishinaabe have thousands of stories to help people bloom. We've heard many of them growing up. And you know why they are effective?"

"Why?" Lulu asks.

"Because many times, we use animals to tell them. We

speak of wolves, moose, bears, eagles, foxes, snakes, and bees. Those animals become real in our head. They teach us lessons. Real life lessons. So, I used our ancestors' methods to help you. These animals became your audience. They became real and became part of your story. You've always had an audience, because your ancestors are always with you. Sometimes we forget that. These animals here were just to remind you that you're never alone."

How does a twelve-year-old girl know so much? Is it because her father is a chief and she was raised learning all about our Ojibwe culture? That's so strange to me. I was raised on Nickelodeon and *Sesame Street*.

"But how did they move? I saw them move. That bunny. It was dancing," Lulu says.

Whoa. She saw them moving too. But wait . . . Dancing? Did she really see them dancing?

"Music is magic, and that magic moved the crowd," Niimi continues. "Now all you've got to do when you're singing in front of people, is see them as a bunch of animals. After a few performances, you'll no longer care who or what they are. You'll only care about one thing—making them move," Niimi says.

"What if she doesn't believe in magic?" I interrupt. "What if they were just off balance and fell over? Maybe the wind moved an ear or tail. But it wasn't magic." I shrug. "It was just music."

"Can you see music? Taste music? Touch music?" Niimi asks. "No. It's weightless. Odorless. Invisible. And yet it can break a heart and melt a heart and put a heart back together for millions of people in a matter of two minutes. If that's not magic, I don't know what is."

"So, my stage fright is dead?" Lulu asks, rushing up and hugging her.

"Your stage fright isn't dead. But the superhero inside of you is now challenging the villain to a fight. But you must keep playing. The more you play, the more you fight. The more you fight, the more you bloom," Niimi says through the hug.

Then she slips out of her pig costume and tosses it to me. I remove the turkey garb and place them both on the couch. I follow Niimi outside, and we walk to our bikes.

I need to process what just happened. I need to think logically here. All Niimi did was give Lulu a way to not think about her fear. It wasn't supernatural. It was simply a friendly game of manipulation. She tricked her. She's making Lulu think that her fear was an enemy that needed to be defeated, when really all Lulu needed was a cute little distraction to make her forget about being afraid. Maybe that's all that this Native boot camp really is. A distraction from reality. Maybe she's distracting me right now. I can't steal if I'm off pulling stunts like this all day. Boot camp, my butt! She's just keeping me busy so I don't raid the mall.

Little does she know that a thief will always find a way to steal. The joke's on them. And I have a microphone in my backpack to prove it.

"There was someone in the crowd you were trying to avoid," Niimi says as she climbs onto her bike.

"Someone in the crowd?" I laugh. "They were stuffed animals."

"I watched you. There was one section of the audience you refused to look at. I'd like to know why," she insists.

Ugh. I don't know how she was able to pick up on that. She'll make me pretend the bear is my best friend or something. But Niimi can't change me, no matter how convincing her charade is . . . It's still a charade. I see through her mask.

And that weird daydream of me getting punched in the face never really happened. It was just a blip of feeling guilty, but now that feeling's gone. I feel fine.

"You're not ready to talk about the makwa yet . . . That's okay," Niimi says.

"I have no clue what you're talking about. In fact, everything that happened back there, that was—"

"Awesome?" Niimi tries to finish my sentence.

"No. You convinced a singer to sing. Big wow. What's next? You going to convince a comedian that he's funny?" I say.

"Still in denial, I see. That's okay. I expected as much from you," she says.

"Oh yeah, and why's that?"

"Because, Benny . . . You're a slow learner. Like how your dad was," she says, and rides off, leaving me in Lulu's yard.

A quick burst of anger flares through me. I'm nothing like my father. I am a winner, and he is a loser. I must never forget that. "Wait. I don't know how to get back!" I shout.

"You'll figure it out, tough guy!" she yells, and speeds down the street until she wraps around the corner, out of my view.

I get on George's bike and pedal in the direction she rode in. I wonder why she didn't want me to ride with her. Did I offend her? Or is this another one of her tests?

Even though it only took about thirty minutes to get to Lulu's house, it took nearly two hours for me to finally find my way back home. Well, not home, but to my dad's house. I hop off the bike and quietly sneak it back into the garage. They can hardly call me a thief for it, I mean, I am returning it—but I should sell it soon, before someone else steals it.

George is standing in the Australia section of the living room, holding a book. He sees me and rolls his eyes.

"What are you reading?" I ask.

"Nothing," he says, and puts it back on the shelf.

I see the book before he pushes it in, blending it with all the rest. The cover has a huge hairy spider on it. "*Australia's Deadliest Animals*, huh?"

"Wow. You can read. I owe my mom ten bucks," George says.

"Didn't they make this cute little travel room for you, to try to snap you out of your funk?" I ask.

"What's your point?"

"How in the world would that book ever make you want to go to Australia?" I ask.

"Maybe, unlike you, I'm not afraid of spiders," George says.

"Right, you're only afraid of sunshine and fresh air," I say.

George doesn't like that. He puffs out his chest and walks up to me.

"Say that to my face," he says, and each word sends tiny little spit missiles onto my face.

"I would say, 'You wanna take this outside?' but I know you're too scared to step—" But before I can finish my sentence, George throws a quick jab, hitting me directly in my nose—the exact same spot where Lulu hit me in my strange daydream.

My head jolts back. But unlike the daydream, I don't lose my footing and fall. My adrenaline kicks in, and I charge him, wrapping my arms around his body. I lift him up and slam him against the wall.

Something breaks and crashes to the floor with us. We must have traveled quite a distance, an ocean to be exact, because while we're wrestling on the floor, we end up all the way in Japan by the time we stop. Bamboo shelves, tiny ninja figurines, and cherry blossoms are scattered everywhere.

Before George can pound my head into Tokyo, Wendy barges into the room and yanks him off me. "What the hell is going on? I want answers now!" Wendy shouts at us.

"Nothing. We were just messing around," George says.

I think for a moment, realizing it's far better for the both of us if I agree with him.

"Yeah. He was just showing me some karate moves in Japan. Sorry," I say.

She takes a hard look at George, then back to me. She knows we're lying. "Well, since you're so buddy-buddy now, then you can clean up this mess together. Another stunt like this, and no video games for a week." She points to George. "And you"—she turns to me—"your mother will be notified next time. Along with that handsome judge!"

Why do they keep saying that? "He wasn't even that good-looking!" I say.

Wait. Does Wendy talk to my mom too? That's wrong on so many levels. You don't speak to the home wrecker. You hate them forever. Maybe my dad told Wendy about Judge Mason. But why would he mention that? This isn't Grand Portage; this is straight-up Grand Pour Out Everyone's Business. No one minds their own around here!

Wendy walks out of the room. George and I look at each other. He probably wants to finish what he started, but instead, he starts laughing. And so do I. I guess it is pretty funny. Two boys fighting all over the world.

"You leveled Japan like Godzilla, dude. Not cool," he says.

"I think a temple fell and hit me in the temple," I add, while rubbing my head. "And for the record, you didn't win. You sucker punched me."

"Keep telling yourself that, Benny-hana," he snaps back, in between his laughs.

"Whatever. Where does all this stuff go?" I ask.

George begins to clean up the mess. I scoop up all the fallen ninjas from the floor. A few moments pass. I'm not sure what to say. "So . . . you never leave the house, like, at all?" I ask.

"I don't really want to talk about it," George says.

"Okay, but what about school?"

"I was homeschooled last year. But that got expensive. My mom tries to teach me, but now I mostly do online classes," he says.

"Don't you miss other kids?" I ask. "Why don't you just take the bus? Buses are safe."

"You know what else starts with *B-U-S*? *Business*. So, why don't you mind your own?"

Wasn't I just complaining about people sticking their nose in other people's business? And here I am, sticking mine into his. But to be fair, he punched me in mine, so I deserve a few answers.

Still, I take the hint, get up, and head into the garage. If annoying him gets me out of cleaning, well, then I did my job.

I close the garage door and wonder for the fiftieth time what the heck I'm doing here. I could be home, hitting the malls with my friends, making money. Where's the drill sergeant? Where's Dr. Phil? Where's the family intervention or the cops who take you to visit a jail to show you how awful it is there in an attempt to scare you straight? Where is this stupid boot camp?

Instead I'm forced to watch a masked girl pretend to heal people. I can't believe Lulu fell for that stuffed animal stunt. Sure, it would be super cool if magic was real. But it's not. I thought my dad would magically appear for me every birthday and Christmas . . . But it never happened.

Believing in magic will only let you down.

People like Tommy Waterfalls don't change. They just learn how to hide it better. I just need to expose him.

I wait to hear George's bedroom door shut before I venture back into the living room. All three watch dogs are now sleeping in Jamaica, underneath a Bob Marley poster. I sneak past them and make my way down the hall. My dad's office door is shut. I don't know where he is, but if he was home, he probably would have come out when George and I had our scuffle. If I'm going to do this, now is the time.

I open his door and walk in. It's like a sleeping zoo. Dozens of animals, some painted some not, lie perfectly still in their ceramic poses as I approach his desk. I open his desk drawers and rifle through them. There're Post-it notes, stamps, pens, markers, glue, carving knives, rubber bands, coins, and takeout menus . . . But no signs of alcohol.

At home he didn't even attempt to hide it, but here he has Wendy, and I doubt he wants to lose her like he lost my mom, so I just need to think like him. He thinks everything is a joke, so his stash must be somewhere he thinks is clever or witty. Hmm . . . Where can it be? Maybe behind a ceramic deer? *Deer* rhymes with *beer*. That's clever. I check behind the deer, but nothing . . . Maybe the moose? *Moose* sounds like *booze*. Nope. How about the rhinoceros? Wine-oceros? I peer behind each one but come out empty-handed each time.

"It's extinct," a voice says from behind me.

I turn around and see my dad standing there, arms crossed, eyes disappointed. All three dogs are at his feet, staring at me. They must have told on me. They're nothing but big rats after all.

"What is?" I ask, buying time to come up with an excuse as to why I am snooping around in his office.

"The western black rhino. It went extinct in 2011," he says. "Very sad, isn't it?"

"How?" I ask.

I look at the rhino sculpture. It looks gentle, strong, and overall harmless, despite its horns.

"There are some people who believe the ivory from their horns has medicinal powers," he says.

"I believe those people are called idiots," I say.

"Doing something wrong only makes you an idiot if you know what's right and continue to do wrong. If they don't know it's wrong, they're not idiots. They just need help. I know what I did wrong, Benny. I am no idiot. I learned from my past. No matter how hard you search this house, you won't find what you're looking for," he says, and begins to walk away.

No. He doesn't get to be the perfect role model now. Where was this guy when I needed him? The air in my lungs becomes steam. Angry steam. He doesn't get the last word. Why are my hands shaking? Or are my legs shaking so much that they're rattling my hands?

As he reaches the door, I can't help myself. "But you are an idiot," I say.

He stops but doesn't turn around for another three seconds. He commands his dogs to leave the room. They obey him and go back to their vacation. My dad finally turns to me and looks me in the eyes. "Give it to me. You've earned that."

My stomach drops. I've wanted to say so much to him for years. I've wanted to scream at him. I've pictured his face every time I would punch my pillow. But now I can't find the words. I can't even open my mouth.

"Ikidon," he says. "Say it. You need to release it from your body, son."

I take a deep breath and let it out. "Only an idiot would

leave Mom. Only an idiot would throw everything away. Only an idiot would forget that he has a—"

"Son. I never forgot about you, Benjamin," he says, using my first name for the first time in a very long time. "I left *for* you. I was toxic, and I didn't want you to see me like that anymore. It killed me every day you had to see your father like that. I needed to leave. You deserved better."

"You were my dad. Dads aren't supposed to bail on their family. They are supposed to be there," I say, choking on my words. "E-even when it's hard."

"You're right. I let you down. I let your mother down. I let myself down. You may not see it now, but leaving was the best way to protect you and your mother. I was in a bad place. And the thought of dragging my family down with me scared me. So, when your mother asked me to leave, I did. I wasn't strong enough to stay and work through it. But never once did I forget about you. I just needed to get my life back into a good place before I reached out to you. You don't need to be sneaking around searching for the past. That man is long gone. I lost your mother, but you didn't lose me. I'm right here," he says.

I feel the tsunami rise somewhere from my gut and engulf my throat. I close my mouth to dam it, and the surge shoots north, stinging my injured nose and pushing against my eyes. I have seconds to escape before it all pours out of me. I tilt my head back slightly. "Too late," I say, and rush past him.

As our bodies nearly touch, the dam breaks and tears flood down my face. I look away and bury my face into my hands as I run out of his room, down the hall, and into the living room.

I stop and take in all the countries surrounding me. My dad did all this for George, who isn't even his son. He did this for Wendy, to make her happy, and he already had a wife he was supposed to make happy. He may have "straightened" his life out, but he still abandoned the people who loved him. He doesn't deserve happiness and, most of all, forgiveness. He is still the villain, no matter how many times he pretends to be the hero.

I want to go home. I want to run out of this house and never see it again. I never want to see my dad, Wendy, or George again. They don't need me or want me. They have each other. All I need right now is the only thing that makes me feel special. I need to steal something again. Right now. I need to remind myself I am better than him. I am not weak. I can walk into a store empty-handed and come out with my hands full. That's my superpower.

I rush into the garage, and grab George's bike. I need to find my way back to the mall. It was far, but I don't care. The thought of shoplifting already gets my blood pumping and my heart beating faster. I choose a direction that feels vaguely familiar and pedal as hard as I can away from the house. Away from my dad. Away from all of this.

CHAPTER 16

THE STOLEN COMPASS

I hide George's bike behind a bush. Finding this place wasn't easy. I had to pedal down the highway for three and a half hours. The only way I knew I'd get there eventually was keeping Lake Superior at my side.

Usually, security keeps a close eye on a kid wearing a backpack, but at a trading post like this, I haven't even gotten a second glance. I feel like a wolf strolling through acres of farmland, looking at all the beautiful, delicious sheep. The only question is, what do I want to steal? The truth is, I don't need anything. I just want to prove to my dad that nothing he can do will change me.

I don't need him. I don't need anyone.

I walk past the first set of stores, but none of them interest me. It's all Native American jewelry, dream catchers, and woven blankets with traditional patterns. All that stuff looks expensive and is pretty cool, but kids back in Duluth wouldn't buy it. I need to steal something I can sell. Rule number five.

I take the stairs up to the second floor and see a small store that sells hunting gear and camping stuff.

Jackpot! People in Duluth love to go camping. I can stuff my backpack with binoculars, hunting knives, camouflage hats, and walkie-talkies. I put on my most curious customer expression and approach the store—but just as my first foot crosses the threshold, an all-too-familiar voice calls out from behind me. "Not another step, Benjamin Waterfalls."

I turn around, and it's Niimi, sipping on a hot cocoa. She may not know there's whipped cream around the fabric over the tip of her nose, and I'm not going to tell her.

"Are you following me?" I ask.

"Technically, I was here first. I didn't think you'd take so long. But it did give me time to get us hot cocoas. Here." She reveals another cup from behind her back and offers it to me.

"How did you know I'd come here?" I ask, and take the warm drink from her.

I don't want to accept it, because I'm on a mission and this is just another attempt at distracting me, but it's so cold outside and I don't remember the last time I had a hot cocoa, so I do.

"You're upset. And I know why you're here," she says.

"Oh, right. Because superheroes know everything. I forgot?" I say, and take a sip.

It glides down my throat, smiling and singing the entire way to my stomach.

"I know that you shouldn't go in there and steal. I know the guy working there. His name is Sam Morrison. He and his family are super sweet. They grew up on the rez, and they're pooling all their income to send their younger sister, Lavinia, off to college. If inventory is off, he'll have to answer for it," Niimi says.

I look at the guy at the register. He's a teenager with spiky black hair and glasses, wearing a camouflage shirt that says YOU CAN'T SEE ME on it.

I was so excited to steal, but this girl completely ruined the vibe. Now I'd feel bad for getting this nerd busted for sleeping on his watch. This sucks. Why can't people just leave me alone?

"Don't you have someone else to rescue? I mean, you believe you're a superhero, right? Go do superhero stuff and leave me alone," I say.

She laughs. "If I wasn't here to swoop in and save the day, some thief would have rolled in and robbed the place. Sam would be fired, Lavinia would have to delay her college plans, and the family-owned store would have lost money. I totally just did superhero stuff."

I never really thought about what happens after I leave a store. Do employees really get held accountable? Does it come out of their paychecks? That's so unfair. Everyone knows people steal. It's part of life. I wonder how many people I got in trouble. Maybe even got fired?

"Look, you stopped me from stealing. You happy?"

"I am. For Sam, I am," she says.

"Good, Dr. Seuss. Now you can leave. I believe, I believe, that now you can leave," I say, mimicking her. "Unless . . . you're being paid to babysit me. Are you?"

"I'm not here to babysit you, but I am working. Now, after you finish your hot cocoa, we can get down to business. There's someone out there waiting for us, and I don't like being late," Niimi says.

"What? Who's waiting for us?" I ask.

Maybe this is finally the start of the real boot camp? I wonder who is out there, the angry drill sergeant or the kindly Dr. Phil type of therapist who will make me get in touch with my inner feelings and admit that stealing is bad. I'm secretly hoping for the drill sergeant. I'm sick of feelings. I just wanna be forced to run a dozen laps, drop and give him twenty, then finally go home.

"Follow me," she says, and walks off.

I sip the hot cocoa and follow her outside and see a man near a large black pickup truck waiting for her. He is a bald white man and has a large gut overflowing out of his shirt.

This must be the drill sergeant. Hello, boot camp. No more silly games and talk of magic and superheroes. The sooner boot camp starts, the sooner it'll be over, which means the sooner I can put all this behind me.

We approach him, and up close, I can see the heavy bags under his eyes. His camouflage pants and scuffed-up black boots fit the setting well, but he's wearing a neon orange shirt, which completely contradicts his pants. His top half says *look at me*. His bottom half says *you can't see me*. Seriously? You want to be seen or not?

"This is him?" the guy asks, with a tinge of disappointment in his voice.

"In the flesh," Niimi says to him, then whispers to me, "Just go along with everything I say.

"Benny, this is Hank. Hank, this is Benny."

"He doesn't look like an expert to me," Hank says. "I mean, he looks more like one of those scrawny street thugs who stole my radio out of my truck last week."

I know I should be offended, but I'm not. One, because he's right. I have stolen many radios out of trucks back in Duluth, and two, because drill sergeants are supposed to be mean. I just thought it would be from a tough-looking Native man, one with scars across his chest and a deep thunderous voice, not an overweight white guy who wears contradicting clothes.

Whatever. Let's just get this over with.

"Could have been him. Buckshot Benny here hunts many things. I'm sure radios are just one of his many prey, ain't that right?" she says, and looks at me.

Umm . . . "That's right. I can't deny hunting down a few radios from time to time," I say.

"Well, if you think this will work, let's go. Alex is waiting," Hank says, and smacks his truck.

As he walks around to the driver's side, I see a young kid, maybe seven years old, sitting in the back seat. "I'm confused," I whisper to Niimi.

"This next blooming of mine is quite a unique one. I'm kind of working as a double bloomer. I need you to keep the boy distracted when we reach the woods. Just talk to him about stuff. Except for stealing. I need enough time alone with the dad for this to work," she says.

"Wait. I thought we were going to finally begin my boot camp. This is just another gig of yours?"

"You help me with this, and I'll boot you into boot camp myself. Okay?"

"Fine. I'll distract the kid. What about George's bike?"

"Toss it in the back," Niimi says.

I run over to the bush and grab George's bike. Hank takes it from me and puts it in the bed of his truck. That was nice of him. He's definitely not a drill sergeant.

"First, we're going to make a quick stop back at Lulu's," Niimi says. "When we get there, run in and tell her you need to borrow a stuffed animal. Grab the wolf and put it in your backpack. Don't let Hank see it. When you're alone with Alex, give it to him. He'll do the rest."

I can't believe Hank trusts the word of a kid in a mask. I wonder how much he's paying her.

Niimi hops into the truck. I follow her in and take the back seat, next to Alex. He looks anxious. He wears the same outfit as his father, but that's their only similarity. Hank is huge, and Alex, well, he's so thin and fragile-looking that I bet the wind could knock him over.

"Hi," I say to him.

"So, you're the thief, huh?" he whispers to me.

Even the kids catch the wind super quickly around here. I nod.

We drive out of the parking lot and enter the highway, heading north. On the floorboard, by my feet, I see a compass sticking out of a small black leather travel bag. The compass is gold plated, with a large moose carved into it. And just like that, my blood begins to heat up and race through my body. I want it. And if I want it, it will be mine. No one ever gave me a compass, so it's my job to give it to myself. They won't even know I attacked. I'm that good. I make sure no one is looking and slip my hand down toward it. With my eyes still on Alex, I pluck it out of the bag and stuff it between my legs, then make it look like I'm tying my shoe.

When the truck stops, I make a smooth movement and

cup the compass into my hand and grab my backpack. As I open the door, I drop it into my backpack and step out. I could probably sell this for at least twenty bucks back home. Everyone needs direction.

At Lulu's I get the stuffed wolf and shove it into my backpack. She doesn't ask any questions, barely looks up from her guitar. Some rock star.

We keep driving until we can't see the sky through the trees. The road ends at a campground. What the heck are we doing here?

We exit the truck. Hank slaps his arm around his son. "Alex. This guy here is going to tell you what I've been trying to get through to you this whole time. Okay?"

Alex shrugs. "If you say so, Dad."

"You'll see. It's a man thing. Over time, you won't even think about it. It will just be as natural as breathing air. Ain't that right?" he says, and looks at me.

He thinks I'm going to side with him, but little does he know that I don't like dads. But I also can't blow Niimi's cover for whatever cockamamie plan she concocted.

"Well, it's a little more complicated than that, pops," I say.

The father looks at me like I'm a puzzle he'll never finish. Niimi laughs out loud. "Buckshot Benny is right. Hunting is nothing like breathing air. And if you want your son to ever become a master hunter like you, you can't go filling his head with such wacky comparisons."

"I just meant—"

"I'm sure you meant well, but let the expert handle this." Niimi flicks her hand at me, which can only mean that it's my cue to take Alex deeper into the woods and allow her to work her so-called magic.

Hunting. So that's what this is about. I'm supposed to pretend to be a master hunter. This guy wants his kid to kill things. The only hunting I know is merchandise hunting. I steal stuff, not lives. This ought to be interesting. I can't wait to see how Niimi pulls this off.

"See you manipu-later," I shout to Niimi, and hope she catches my dig at her. "Let's go, Alex," I say, and walk off. Alex follows, kicking up dirt with each step.

"Don't you need the rifle?" Hank shouts to us as we stroll down a hunting trail.

"Ninety percent of hunting is mental. Let them reach the first ninety before we go handing the guns out," Niimi says.

I take Alex far away enough where we can no longer hear or see Niimi and Hank. I'm not sure what she wants me to do or what she wants me to say, so I turn to Alex.

"So, what's the deal between you and your dad?" I ask.

"He wishes I was more like him," Alex says.

"Well, one way to do that is to eat nonstop," I say. "He's pretty fat."

Alex laughs. "He says I'll never be a man unless I start acting like one."

"Sometimes dads suck. Sorry, but it's true."

"Does your dad want you to kill animals too?" Alex asks.

"Mine sucks in other ways. Maybe you can just tell yours that you don't want to kill animals."

"I've tried. He never listens to me," Alex says. "That's why Niimi is here. That's why you're here."

"I don't even know why I'm here," I say. "I'm supposed to be in some boot camp to stop stealing, instead I'm walking around the forest with a scrawny little kid—no offense," I say.

"It's okay. But I do know why you're here. You're the decoy. Right now, Niimi is not making me more like my dad, but making my dad more like me," he says.

"How do you know that?" I ask.

"My dad asked for her help, but secretly, I paid her eight dollars to help me instead. Now give me the wolf," he says.

Niimi took money from this kid. And she calls me a thief?

I pull the wolf out of my backpack. He removes his orange shirt, and under it is a gray shirt with a white patch near the belly. It's long-sleeved and bunched up at his elbows. He rolls the sleeves down to his wrist and flips up the hood. Two fabric-stuffed wolf ears pop up on the hood. I bet Niimi got him that while she was getting the turkey and pig costumes. He then reaches into his pocket and pulls out a piece of coal. "Coal?" I ask.

"It's my nose," he says, and rubs it against his nose, making it as black as a wolf's nose.

"I heard it's pretty dangerous to dress up as a wolf and play in the woods, especially with people like your dad around," I say.

"I trust Niimi," he says, and takes the wolf from my hands.

There's that word again: *trust*. What an annoyingly common word that has been lately.

"Go back to my dad and Niimi. Tell them I found a wolf," Alex interrupts my thoughts.

"Nah, I don't think leaving you alone dressed up like this is a good idea. I don't care if you trust Niimi or not, and neither do bullets," I say.

"Niimi planned this out already. Just go," Alex says.

"Niimi is just a kid a few years older than you. And look at me. Would you put your life in my hands? No. Plus, Niimi wears a mask and believes in superheroes. She probably believes in Santa too," I say.

His eyes open wide. His eyebrows rise. "Are you saying Santa isn't real?" he asks.

Crap. Forgot the kid is so young. Kids are supposed to believe in that stuff.

"No. Santa is real. Obviously. I just meant maybe we shouldn't put all this faith in a girl who only shows half of her face. That's all," I say.

"The Flash only shows half of his face, and so does Captain America. I trust them. Now, go," he says, and kneels down and gets on all fours, placing the wolf to face him.

I walk back to where the truck is parked, leaving Alex with his stuffed wolf. I feel bad for him. I know what it feels like to want your dad to be your hero, even when he proves otherwise.

When I reach Niimi and Hank, they both look at me like I'm missing an arm.

"Where's Alex?" Hank asks.

"He found something to shoot," I say.

Hank's eyes light up. "Really?" he says, and grabs his rifle, which is leaning against the truck.

"Well, what are we waiting for?" Niimi asks. I see her mischievous grin. Her plan is working.

Hank, Niimi, and I walk quietly back to where Alex is. We step carefully over the ground, trying not to snap twigs and crush leaves too loudly.

I have no idea what's going to happen, but I feel uneasy about how excited this man is. "Be ready," Niimi whispers into Hank's ear.

He nods and softens his footsteps. "Alex?" he whispers two or three times as we tiptoe farther. "Where is he?"

"I see the ma'iingan," Niimi says, and points left. "That means wolf."

Hank whips the barrel toward the left. In his sights, he sees his son, dressed as a wolf, on all fours, innocently playing with the stuffed wolf. His eyes widen.

"What the . . . ," Hank says under his breath.

"Tell me what you see," Niimi whispers into his ear.

"I see my boy."

"What is he doing?" Niimi asks.

"Playing," he says as he slowly lowers his rifle.

"What else do you see?" she asks.

"I see . . . a wolf. A baby wolf."

Wait. What? He should see a stuffed animal, shouldn't he? I do.

"With one bullet, you can take away both childhoods."

"What?" Hank says, and looks at Niimi with confusion tugging at his forehead.

"Your father taught you to hunt, didn't he?"

"Yes," Hank says.

"When you were your son's age, did you want to kill animals?" Niimi asks.

Hank pauses. "What's going on?"

"Your innocence was shot dead in a forest just like this, wasn't it?" she says.

"I don't . . . remember. I don't know."

"But you do remember, Hank. You do. When you were Alex's age, did you want to kill animals?"

He looks down, near his feet, remembering his childhood . . . "No. I was . . . like my son. I didn't want to do it."

"Please don't make me shoot it, Daddy. Please," Niimi says, causing more of Hank's memories to flood back.

Hank opens his mouth. But words don't come out. Just a deep breath he's been holding ever since he was a kid. "Alex says the same thing to me. My God. I've turned into my dad."

"Maybe your dad was wrong, and you were right. Maybe your son is right. Maybe we're not here to teach him; perhaps your son is here to teach you," Niimi says.

Hank looks at Alex, who plays with the stuffed wolf, but Niimi and Hank aren't seeing what I am seeing. I see Alex bouncing and hopping around the toy. Nothing out of the ordinary. Kids do that, right? But Hank sees something different. I can tell by the tears ganging up on his eyes, ready to unload on him.

"You're seeing what I'm seeing, right?" I ask them both.

"It's a pup. With my boy," Hank says, and begins to cry—probably recalling all the wolves he shot and killed for fun.

He sees a wolf. Just like how Lulu saw real animals in her house. This is impossible. Am I missing something? All I see is a kid playing with a toy. But Niimi sees it too. I just know it. The way she's smiling. Does Alex see it? Does he think he's actually playing with a real baby wolf? Can someone please tell me what the flip is going on?

Hank drops to his knees, sets his gun down, and stares at his little boy.

"He doesn't need a hunter. He needs a father," Niimi says.

"Alex!" Hank shouts.

At the sound of his voice, the wolf turns its head, stiffens its ears, looks at us, and falls over. Okay . . . that was a little strange, but again, the wind could have blown it over.

"Dad!" Alex shouts back to his dad, rising to his feet and running toward his father.

They meet in the middle and embrace each other. Both squeezing tightly, and from the looks of it, it's a hug they both have been wanting and needing from one another for a very long time. Right then, I realize I have not had a hug like this since before my dad left. I was so young then, as young as Alex. But I still remember it. How it smelled. How warm it was. How safe and protected I felt.

Hank releases his son and looks at Niimi. "Not exactly what I had in mind, but thank you, Niimi."

"You wanted your son to be strong," she says. "That's what you got."

What are they talking about? Why is everyone acting like something huge just happened? I look over at the stuffed wolf, but it's gone. There's no trace of it.

"Where'd the wolf go?" I ask.

"Didn't you see it run off?" Alex asks me.

"No. Of course not," I say, frustrated that everyone is in on this except me.

Niimi walks up to Alex. He hugs her. "Raise this big guy well," she says.

"I will," he replies as he stares at his father with hopeful eyes.

"Let's go home." Hank takes his son's hand, and they walk back to the truck.

I turn to Niimi. "What just happened?" I ask.

"A boy just became a man, and a man just became a dad."

"And the wolf? You're telling me they saw a real wolf?"

"They saw what they needed to see to bring them together. You saw what you wanted to see," Niimi says. "Plus, killing wolves is illegal in Minnesota. I knew he wouldn't listen to the law, so I found a better way to reach him."

"Through his son? You tricked him."

"Telling a father to pay closer attention to his son is not a trick. It's an act of kindness."

"Kindness? To who?"

"Well, for one, the wolf. And his son, and to him. Everybody wins when he puts down the gun."

"And just like that, he's no longer a hunter? Come on," I say.

"No, Hank has a long road ahead of him. He's been a hunter his whole life. He's only been a nonhunter for about a minute. But the superhero in him is awake. Now they fight," she says. "It's up to him who wins."

I am getting pretty tired of this silly superhero talk. It

doesn't take superpowers to tell someone killing animals is wrong. Why is everyone falling for this girl's tricks?

"You guys coming?" Hank shouts back to us.

"No. We still got some work to do," Niimi says back.

"We do?" I ask. "I need to get George's bike."

"Don't worry about the bike. Hank knows where to put it."

"Put it? Why are we not going back with them?" I ask.

"You thought you were the decoy to get me alone with Hank, but maybe they were the decoy the whole time. Maybe I just wanted to get you alone in the woods."

I look around. I have no idea where we are, or even which direction is home. All I do know is that Niimi somehow planned this. She kept me from stealing and got me into the middle of the forest. And our ride just left. But why does she want me out here?

"No more games. How do we get home?" I ask, but she doesn't answer me with words. Instead, her feet answer me. She starts walking.

CHAPTER 17

LOST IN THE TREES

After a lot of walking, I notice that everywhere we've been looks exactly the same. "Do you even know where you're going?" I finally ask Niimi.

"Forward. Always forward. Never backward, Benny."

"Yeah. So . . . in other words, we're lost?" I ask.

"It appears that way. Doesn't this tree look exactly like the tree we walked by twenty minutes ago?" she asks.

I'm a city kid. I can do sketchy neighborhoods and dark alleys, but I feel totally out of my element in forests. And I hate feeling out of my element. Especially when there are wild animals around.

"Niimi! It's going to get dark soon!"

She laughs. "If only . . ."

"If only what?" I snap back.

She gives me the side-eye. "If only . . . we had a way of knowing which direction we were going."

My stomach tightens. That's impossible. I made sure no one was looking. Especially her. She was in the front seat. How could she possibly know I took it? Unless . . . "Holy crap! You totally set me up!" I shout.

"Set you up? Did I plant it in your backpack?" she asks.

"No. But you knew I'd take it," I say.

"No one knew you would take it, except you," she says.

"You walked me right into this trap. I should have never come to Grand Portage!"

"Your father said the same thing, many times, until the day he said coming here was the best thing he's ever done."

"Stop it! I'm not my dad. I'm nothing like him. And you know nothing about me, so just shut up and show me the way out of this stupid forest!" I shout even louder.

She thinks her blooming stuff is going to work on me. Well, it won't. If she wants to get personal, then I can too . . .

"Forget my dad," I say. "I want to talk about why you wear that mask."

Her eyes turn wild. "Why did you take the compass?" she asks through her teeth.

"You tell me. You pretend to know all the answers. Or do I have to pay you first?"

She growls. "Tell me why you took the compass!"

"What does it matter?"

"Because everything we do matters. What we choose to

do determines who we choose to be. Why did you take the compass?" she repeats.

"Because I'm a thief! That's all I am. Without stealing, I am nothing!" I shout so loud that it sends birds launching out of the trees and taking to the sky. "You satisfied?" I ask her. "Forget it. Here's your damn compass!" I say, and pull it out of my bag. I hold it out to her, but her hands stay at her waist.

"You stole it. It's yours now," she says. "Isn't that how it works?"

"I was just gonna sell it when I left this place. But if you need it to get us out of here, then take it!"

"I don't need it. I know exactly where we are," she says, and walks off.

Another test? I'm so sick of this. "Oh, so you just lied this entire time about being lost? Just like how you lie about everything else. You trick them all into believing they can be superheroes. But I bet Lulu is still afraid to sing. Hank will still want to kill animals. Alex still won't like his dad. People don't bloom! What you sold them is a lie. And that makes you not a superhero, but a villain," I shout as she walks, but . . . She stops, turns around, and approaches me.

Her eyes look aflame. "People do bloom. But you have to be brave enough to do it. Like your dad. Believe it or not, he's a changed man. The only one refusing to learn from their mistakes is you," she says.

"At least I'm not the one hiding my face from the world.

I mean, are you ever gonna take off that ridiculous mask? Shouldn't you have grown out of playing that silly superhero game by now? What are you, five?"

"You want to see my superpower, Benny?"

"You have none," I say. "Superheroes are something only losers believe in because it distracts them from the truth. And the truth is, life sucks. They look for someone else to solve their problems, but news flash, Niimi, we are walking, talking skin bags full of blood, bones, and problems. At least I'm brave enough to admit that."

"You are many things, but brave is not one of them," she says, and shoves me in the chest.

"At least I'm not afraid to show my face," I say.

"Sure, you are. You just mask it in other ways."

"Is that your superpower? Just saying catchy little bumper sticker phrases all the time?"

"No, this is my superpower," she says, and *CRACK!*

Niimi lands a crisp left cross. It hits me in the freakin' exact spot George and Lulu hit me in. My nose stings. My knees buckle. I fall back, and my head slams onto the ground.

Lights out.

"Wake up, Benny Bear."

Seconds pass. Maybe minutes. I have no idea. I open my eyes, and my vision immediately blurs. Did she seriously just hit me? I jolt from the thunder that loudly cracks above my head and rolls across the sky. Oh, no. Where there's thunder comes rain. Niimi steps forward and stands over me. She removes her mask, but my vision is too blurry to make out her face. "Niimi? Is that you?" I ask, trying to clear my eyes by rubbing them.

Lightning strikes a tree near us, sending sparks everywhere. I watch them fall down to the ground like electric raindrops. And when I look back to Niimi, she is gone.

"Niimi?"

I try to stand up—whoa, I'm a bit dizzy. Forget bloomer, that girl should be a boxer. I look in all directions but see only trees. Then it begins to rain. Oh, no. This can't be happening. More thunder growls above me, like hungry sky hounds searching for a meal. They shake the trees back and forth, causing birds to escape and squirrels to scurry away. This is legit scary. I need to get the heck out of this forest.

"Niimi? Where are you?" I shout.

"Seriously! I'm lost. Where are you?" I shout even louder.

Niimi is nowhere to be found. All I can hear is howling wind all around me, and the whips of lightning cracking the sky. I can't believe she punched me! I can't believe she left me here. Was this her plan all along? Was there never a boot camp? Was this always just a way to get rid of me? My dad doesn't want me. My mom doesn't want me. No one does. Well screw them. Screw the whole world. I don't need any of them.

"Fine!" I shout. "I don't need you!"

I take a few steps left and stop. I hear something behind me. I whip around but see nothing. This is not funny. There are wild animals out here. I take a few more steps, then see something moving behind the brush. It looks like a large shadow. What the heck is that? I turn in a circle. The hairs on my entire body stand. Fear grabs my throat. Come on! Please just be an overweight beaver or something. Please.

But in front of me, about twenty yards away, I see a freaking bear step out from the bush. I nearly collapse. Bears attack people when provoked. I need to be perfectly still. I wish I'd paid better attention in class when we learned about bears. Am I supposed to run? Stop drop and roll? Or was that for a fire? Am I supposed to wave my arms and yell? Play dead? It stares at me and sniffs the air. It smells me. Its eyes are black and locked on to me. It stands on its two hind legs and roars. Its teeth are so sharp. They'd easily crush my bones.

"Niimi!" I whisper. The bear moves closer toward me, growling and swiping the ground, kicking dirt up into the air. Is it challenging me to a fight?

I give up.

You win.

I think I need to run . . . But my legs won't move. I can't climb a tree. Everyone knows bears are great climbers. I'm screwed. My heart is beating so fast that it feels like it's going to burst out of my chest. It's so close now that I feel its breath heating up my face. I don't want to die. I'm not ready. I close my eyes and whisper, "Somebody please help me," over and over again.

And after about twenty seconds, I am still alive. I peek one eye open, then the other. The bear is gone. I finally release my breath in one huge exhale. Why didn't the bear attack? Why am I not torn into pieces right now? Then I look down, and at my feet is the stuffed bear. The same stuffed bear that got me in trouble. The same stuffed bear Lulu grabbed off the shelf. I drop to my knees, facing the stuffed animal.

I'm exhausted, soaked head to toe, and more confused than I have ever been before. Even more confused than all those nights I'd lie awake, wondering why my dad didn't want me anymore. I can't believe I was almost killed by a bear.

Or was I? Was the bear real? Was it just this stuffed animal, and I am seeing things like Lulu and Hank and Alex?

What does all this mean? I should be relieved the real bear is gone . . . but I'm not. I'm too overwhelmed. I am too scared. Too confused about everything. Too wet. Too cold. Too hungry. Too tired. I just want to go home. I just want my mom to tell me everything's going to be okay, even if it's a lie.

"Okay! You win! I give up!" I shout in all directions.

Oh, no. I'm breaking down. I've officially reached my breaking point. I need my mom. She never left me. She bent over backward her entire life to not only be my mom, but also be my dad after he left. Please don't give up on me, Mom. Everyone else can hate me and think I'm nothing but trouble, but not you, Mom. I just want to curl up in a warm blanket and have her tell me that I am not a failure. I am not a disappointment. I'm still her son, and she still loves me.

Tears pour out like a storm over my face. The guilt of everything I put my mom through rushes down my cheeks in remorseful streams. And the more I cry, the less it rains.

After crying every last drop out of me, I finally get up and see something around the stuffed bear's neck. It's a red ribbon. And attached to the ribbon is a folded note. I unfold it. It reads *Home is W.*

I pull the compass out of my pocket and open it to see where west is. I just need to get out of this forest and get back to my dad's house. At least it's no longer raining. I stuff the bear into my backpack and begin walking.

Too many terrifying minutes later, where I gave nearly every tree a double take and jumped at each little sound, I finally reach the end of the forest, where the roads begin. George's bike is leaning against a tree, waiting for me.

None of this makes sense. Has Niimi been my drill sergeant all along? Am I blooming?

I stuff the compass into my backpack and get onto George's bike. This has been the weirdest day of my life, and I still need to find my way back to my dad's house.

CHAPTER 18

THE MISSING NECKLACE

Two hours later, I finally reach my dad's property. I don't see any animals around, so they must have all been fed and are asleep. Which reminds me of how hungry and tired I am. I'm soaking wet, covered in scrapes and dirt. I'm so exhausted I feel like I could sleep for a thousand nights. I park George's bike in the garage and walk into the living room, hoping to sneak past everyone and make my way to the kitchen. I'm too tired to eat, but too hungry to sleep. I don't know what to do. Maybe I'll just pass out with food in my mouth. I can chew in my dreams.

But as soon as I walk in, I see my dad and Wendy staring at me, both with their arms crossed and both with an expression I am very used to: disappointment.

"What?" I say, and look down to see that I trekked mud

into the house with my dirty wet shoes. "Oh, sorry. I forgot."
I remove my shoes and hold them in my hands. "I'll clean it
up right after I eat," I add, pointing to my footprints.

But Wendy and my dad haven't moved or said a word.
They are like his ceramic animals, standing perfectly still,
with matching expressions. Identical disapproval.

"I know I'm late, but I got lost in the forest," I say.

"Where is it?" my dad says.

"The forest? Literally everywhere outside," I say.

"I know where the forest is, Benjamin. Wendy's necklace. Where is it?" he asks again.

What is he talking about? "How should I know?" I say,
and take a step toward the kitchen, but Wendy steps in front
of me, blocking my path.

"I want it back," she says.

"I don't even know what you're talking about," I reply.

"It was her mother's necklace, Benny," says my dad.

"Oh, and since I'm the thief, I must have taken it, right?"
I say.

Wendy and my dad look at each other, and in unison
say, "Yeah."

"Well, I didn't, so either she lost it or there's another
thief around here."

My dad points to the wall, in between Hawaii and
Jamaica. My eyes follow his finger. It stops on my suitcase,
stranded in the sea. Seriously?

"Why is my—" I sigh. "You're kicking me out?"

"We can't trust you," Wendy says. "And like I said, trust is everything."

"But I didn't take it. I swear."

"You're telling us that you haven't stolen anything since you arrived here?" Wendy asks.

The images of the golden scarf, the twenty-dollar bill, Lulu's microphone, the dragon shirt, Hank's compass all race through my mind. "I wouldn't exactly say that," I say.

"See! He's been thieving right under our noses," Wendy says.

"But I never took anything from this house, I swear!" I plead.

"Liar. You took my bike," George says from the hallway.

"Oh, come on! I borrowed it," I say.

"You took it. Without asking. That's literally the definition of stealing, bro," George fires back.

"He's right. You just lied to us again," Wendy says.

"I brought the bike back, didn't I?" I say.

"After you called Niimi a liar, and a thief, and what else?" my dad asks Wendy.

"A five-year-old. She called. She told us everything," Wendy says.

"You know what! Fine! I want to go home. Tell my mom I finished this stupid boot camp, and we all go our separate ways," I say. "We all win. You get rid of me, and I get rid of you. Deal?"

"This isn't a negotiation, kiddo. You're going back home,

and I already called your mom and told her what you've done," my dad says. "She's very disappointed."

"What the—"

"The rules were clear. And you broke them. And that handsome judge isn't going to be happy seeing you back so soon."

Panic floods my body. This is so unfair. I didn't even take the necklace, and now I'm being punished for it. I didn't steal it . . . Did I? I don't remember taking it. Do I steal so often that I can't even keep track of the things I take? Is that possible?

I can't go back yet. My mom will never forgive me for messing up so quickly again. I need to say something that keeps me here. Just a bit longer. I need to convince these people that I have changed before they send me back. But they won't take my word for it; they need to hear it from someone they do trust . . .

Niimi!

"Talk to Niimi. She'll tell you how much better I'm getting," I plead.

"Did you not hear us? We did talk to her."

"Then let me talk to her. Something happened to me in the forest. Maybe she'll make sense of it."

"What happened to you?" my dad asks.

"I was almost attacked by a bear," I say.

"What?" Wendy gasps.

"But it didn't hurt me. Turns out it was just a stuffed animal," I say, realizing I sound like Niimi right now. "I know that doesn't make sense. But maybe it doesn't have to."

They both look at me, like I said something they've never imagined me saying.

"Look, I'm not saying I'm a good person or anything. I know I suck, but maybe, just maybe the bear didn't attack me because I haven't finished this boot camp thingy yet."

"Did you even get me that scarf, Benjamin? Or did you steal that too?" Wendy asks.

"I stole it. But to be fair, then you stole it from me." I point to my dad.

Wendy and my father both sigh at the same time. "Maybe this has all been a waste of time. Clearly you don't want to change. You're not even letting Niimi help you," my dad says.

"Help me? We spend all day fixing other people's problems. Then, when it comes time to start on me, she punches me in the face, ditches me in the forest, leaving me to die where I'm almost eaten alive by a bear. I feel like I'm losing my mind. I need to know what the heck is going on!" I say.

"Oh, Benny. Your healing started the moment she walked into the bookstore," my dad says.

"The bookstore? What are you talking about? Niimi was in there for me?"

"You think I'd let a thirteen-year-old thief work the cash

219

register? Plus, there are child labor laws. The whole thing was set up by Niimi to see what she was working with," Wendy says.

"Has everyone in this freaking place completely lost their mind? Whatever happened to family interventions or counseling or giving me a belt to the butt when I stole something? But no, you all put your trust into some girl that thinks she's the next Wonder Woman. And since she says I am hopeless, you're all just going to take her word and send me packing?" I ask, realizing my logic took a complete one-eighty. I wanted them to talk to her to see how much better I've gotten, but now I'm trying to convince them to not listen to her.

"And because you stole Wendy's necklace," my dad says.

"I didn't take her damn necklace!" I say.

I need to show them that I've changed, even if I haven't changed as much as they hoped.

I need to talk to Niimi. Maybe my bear encounter will mean something to her. Maybe it will buy me more time. I can't see the judge yet. I can't face my mom, not until she knows I won't let her down again.

"Let's just all think about this for a minute . . . You are sending me back because you don't think I've changed, right?" I ask them. "But if Niimi says I am changing, can I stay a bit longer and finish my boot camp? That way my mom can be happy again and the judge won't have to send me away."

220

My dad and Wendy converse with their eyes, then nod.

"If she says you're changing, then you can stay a bit longer, but Niimi doesn't lie. You have until noon tomorrow to show her you have. If you can't, you're on that bus heading back to Duluth," he says.

"Okay. I need you to take me to her house," I say.

"Before we do that, let's give Wendy back her necklace."

"I took so many things," I say. "But not that."

"That's the problem with being untrustworthy, Benny. Even when you may be telling the truth, no one will believe you," my dad says as he pats me on the shoulder and he and Wendy walk away.

Before going back to his room, George adds, "You were almost attacked by a stuffed animal? You're so weird, dude."

George's words resonate with me. It felt so real. I could have sworn I was almost attacked, but when I said it out loud, it sounded impossible. Just like the things Niimi says all sound impossible. But what if she's telling the truth about all this? What if she really can bloom people? What if it's not all one big magic trick?

I stand there alone, in silence. I let everyone down again. And this time, I am in trouble for something I didn't steal. I guess it doesn't matter. My dad is right; why would they believe me? I need to talk to Niimi. She's probably still really pissed at me, but she's the only way I stay out of that courtroom.

What can I do that would make Niimi think I've

changed? All I've done here is steal from people who were nice to me. But what if . . . I reverse all the things I've done? What if I can unsteal the things I've stolen?

That's it! I can now give all those things back. I will return the compass to Hank. I'll give Lulu her microphone back. This can work. It has to. Clearly that would convince her that I've changed, right? Even if I'm doing it to save my own butt, that doesn't negate the fact that I'm still doing something good. Oh, gawd. I'm using Niimi's logic now.

I walk down the hall to my dad's bedroom. I knock three times and wait. Wendy answers. She's wearing pajamas, and a toothbrush hangs out of her mouth. I know it's evening, but why is she going to bed so early? What is it, eight p.m.? "Let me see your hands," she says.

I show her my hands. "No necklace, no ride," she says, and shuts the door.

What would Niimi do? Well . . . first off, she'd never be in this situation because she's not a thief . . . But . . . if she did find her way into my shoes, I bet she'd look at the bigger picture. I bet she'd walk for hours in a forest pretending to be lost just to teach me a lesson about stealing compasses. Maybe I need to bite the bullet and take the blame for the necklace . . . And later, after I convince Niimi to help me stay, I'll ask her to tell Wendy that I didn't take the necklace in the first place. They'll believe her. Niimi doesn't lie, they said so themselves.

I knock again. Wendy swings the door open. "Can we

help you, Benny?" Wendy asks, stepping to the side, revealing my dad standing there, waiting for my response. All three dogs are on their bed. Wow. It's so much warmer in this room.

"I'll give the necklace back, but only after you take me to see Niimi."

"I don't negotiate with thieves," my dad says.

"Tommy. I want that necklace back. Just take him to see Niimi. He should at least have a chance to say goodbye to her," Wendy says.

Even after she believes I took her necklace, she is still somehow nice to me.

"You take him, I'll wake up early and feed the animals," he replies.

"No. You take him. I'm pretty sure the goats and ducks won't rob me. Benny on the other hand, might try to steal the Jeep while I'm in it."

"Fine. Grab your coat," he says, and walks past me. "The dogs need to go out anyway."

I grab my backpack, a coat, and meet my dad outside. He is still in his pajamas, so he and the three dogs run to his Jeep as if the ground was made of hot coals, which is weird because it's so cold out. Burning freezing icicles . . . Icicles said really slowly . . . *ice-coals*?

The dogs pile into the back. I've heard of people walking dogs, but never heard of people taking their dogs out for a drive. Before he starts the Jeep, he turns to me. "I was in your corner, Benny. Why'd you have to take Wendy's necklace?" he asks.

Even though I didn't, I sigh and say, "You left my corner a long time ago."

I'm still mad at him. He's still mad at me . . . But right now, the only thing that matters is somehow convincing Niimi to not abandon my corner. I need her on my side.

He's so disappointed that he's silent during the entire drive. Since I have arrived in Grand Portage, I couldn't get him to stop talking, but now, a part of me wishes he would say something. Even one of his cheesy jokes. The tension between us is thick, but I need to get in a better mindset if I am going to convince him—and everyone else—to let me stick around for a while.

"Got any more riddles?" I ask. "Maybe a joke about a thief?"

"I'm all out of humor, right now, Benny," he says.

But I know him. Some things never change. And he's been telling jokes since the day I was born. He'll never pass up an opportunity to make someone laugh. Even when he's mad. And even when he's pretending to be fresh out of humor. Whatever that means.

Ten seconds later, he cracks a smile. Yep. I knew it. "Well, I do know one."

"Let's hear it. And don't worry. We can still be mad at each other after the joke," I say.

"Okay. What did I do when the thief broke into my house

while I was sleeping and started searching for money?" he asks.

"I don't know. What did you do?" I ask.

"I woke up and started searching with him," he says, and laughs.

Before I know it, a small chuckle escapes my mouth.

Twenty minutes later, I look out the window and see a small brown house. Not at all what I'd picture for a house with a tribal chief living inside it. "You really came face-to-face with a makwa?" my dad asks.

"Want proof?" I ask, and pull the stuffed bear out of my backpack and hand it to him.

My dad's eyes well up, and he nearly stumbles over his words. "This is the bear you saw?"

"Yeah, why?"

"You don't remember this, do you?" He holds it up to me.

"No. All I know is I freeze up every time it's around me," I say.

"You should hold on to this guy for a while longer. Maybe you'll realize why it keeps popping up on you." He smiles and hands it back to me.

I stuff it into my backpack.

"Have Niimi call me when you need a ride home. And don't be long. It's getting late."

"Okay."

I hop out of the Jeep. He watches me as I walk up to

the house. I'm not sure if he is making sure I'm safe or just waiting to see if I'll try to steal something. Once I enter the property, he drives off with his watch dogs.

I walk up to the house. The sign in front of the yard reads GICHIGAMI GARDEN. The entire front yard is covered in beach glass instead of grass. The ground shimmers from the moonlight, reflecting all the sparkling shards of glass. In the middle of the shiny lawn is a large tree, with dozens and dozens of different colored glass bottles hanging down from the branches on strings. Each bottle has a piece of paper inside. People need a place to hang their messages, I guess. Answering machine? Phone? Send a text? Email? Nope . . . *Beep*. Just leave a message in my tree. It looks like an art installation by some Twin Cities hipster. I wonder what it's for. As I walk under the dangling bottles, I see there are names written on each one.

"That's a whole lot of people to bloom, ain't it?" a voice says from behind me. I turn around and see an older woman with a black dog approach me. A bottle is in her hand, and in the bottle is a note.

She is dressed in a long floral green dress under her brown coat. She must be so cold. Her hair shines in silver. But the way she's moving suggests she's not cold at all. It's almost as if she's gliding to music only she can hear. She looks old, but she's basically dancing her way over the glass. And she keeps her eyes on me, like she's reading my face like a book. Why is she smiling? "Do you live here?" I ask, thinking maybe my dad sent me to the wrong house on purpose in another one of his attempts to be funny.

"Me? No. I'm just passing through. Leaving a note here for a friend of mine who fell on tough times," she says as she ties her bottle to one of the strings hanging down.

"Yeah, times sure can be tough," I say.

"Yes, they can, kiddo. But remember, we're tougher," she says, and gives me a wink. There's something so warm about her. And even though I have no clue who she is, she keeps grinning and staring at me like she knows exactly who I am. "Good luck on your adventure, kid," she says. "Let's go home, Seven," she says to her dog, and walks back toward the street. Her dog follows.

Seven. That's an interesting name for a dog. But this place is full of people with interesting names. Do people travel from all over Minnesota to come here? Does every reservation have a tree like this? Every tribe? I look up at the bottles again and feel the heaviness of so many people hurting. So many cries for help. So many people trying to better themselves. No wonder Niimi's dad asked her to take over this part of the job. There are so many people to help.

I leave the tree and approach the door. The doormat under my feet says ANISHINAABE NIIN. I wonder if that means "home sweet home" in Ojibwe. I knock three times.

CHAPTER 19

NIMAAMAA DIBIKI-GIIZIS [MY MOON MOTHER]

Niimi's father answers the door. He wears a long red bathrobe and his eyes are red, like he's been either reading or crying all day. "Sorry to bother you this late, sir, but is Niimi home?" I ask.

He eyes me suspiciously. "You're Tommy Waterfalls's son, aren't you?"

"I am," I say. "I guess we haven't officially met."

"I'm Stanley Waatese. My daughter's pretty upset. Did you call her a liar?" he asks.

"Yes, and a thief." I take a deep breath. "But I'm here to apologize."

He laughs, which surprises me and is a relief. "Well, in that case, you can come in here and wait. She had to go save the world really quick. But she'll be back soon."

"I'm sorry," I say as I follow him inside the house. "But, saving the world?"

"As you've probably gathered, my daughter chooses to see a marvelous world. You choose to see a marvel-less world. But at the end of the day, a superhero is someone willing to help people who need it," he says and points outside to his tree full of bloom bottles. "It really doesn't matter what you or I or even Niimi choose to call it. As long as we make the world a better place, right?"

He's right. So what if she believes in superheroes? People believe in all sorts of things. I should know. My time here has made me question everything.

"I guess you're right. Maybe a world without heroes leaves us with a world full of villains," I say.

"You sound like Niimi. I see she's rubbing off on you," he says.

Normally, being compared to Niimi would cause me to burst out laughing, but for some strange reason, hearing it from this man, it makes me feel good.

"Is this an Ojibwe thing?" I ask.

"What do you mean, an Ojibwe thing?"

"Everything I've experienced since I arrived," I say. "The blooming and all that?"

"It's a human thing," the chief replies. "When a doctor saves a patient's life, it is called their practice. When a firefighter saves the lives of the people trapped inside a burning house, it is called their duty. When a teacher breaks through to a student, it is called their job. And when we set someone on a mission to become the best version of themselves, we are called Nenaadawi'. You don't have to be Ojibwe to want to take care of people, you just have to be human."

I take in the art on the walls of the living room. There are so many paintings, and the people in them look like Native American warriors. Or I guess Niimi would call them the original superheroes. Some are men, some are women; all are proud-looking. They're beautiful.

There is also a framed photograph of a woman on the shelf, surrounded by colorful beach glass and flowers. I'm guessing this is Niimi's mother. And in the photo, she is wearing the same mask that Niimi wears now.

The chief gestures to the couch, and I take a seat.

The room fills with a silence that makes me feel like I should say something important. "I'm sorry your wife passed away."

He nods and touches her face on the framed photograph. "She's waiting for me, you know? But I can't leave just yet. There's so much more work to do," he says while plopping down on the chair beside me.

"Yeah, I saw your message tree. Looks like you'll be busy for a long time."

"Luckily for me, my wife is a very patient woman. She'll wait for me," he says, and points out the window.

I follow his finger that leads straight to the moon.

"That's where she's waiting for me. On the dibiki-giizis."

230

"Does that mean 'moon'?" I ask.

"No. *Moon* means 'dibiki-giizis.' We were here first," he says, and smiles at me.

I'm starting to understand where Niimi gets her way of looking at things.

"She's up there, watching us now."

"In the moon? I mean, in the dibiki-giizis?" I ask.

"That's right. And at night, when you see fireflies dancing around, those are her kisses. They're on their way to find me," he says. "She's one helluva kisser, that woman."

I wonder if my parents ever loved each other that much. I wonder if George's dad is waiting for him on the moon.

"May I ask what happened?"

"Manijooshiwaapinewin. She fought and won hundreds of battles in life, but all it took was losing one fight to take her away from me."

"I don't know what that means," I admit. There's so much I don't know. "Can I ask you something?"

"You want to know if your father has really changed?" he asks.

"Yes. How did you know?"

"It's what you wanted to know since you arrived. It's all you want to know. It's why you're here."

"He says he has."

"Then he has. You should believe him until you have a reason not to believe him."

Niimi may be like her mom, but she's also so much like

her dad. They look at life like it is a gift. I spend most of mine thinking it's a bag of crap.

"I'm afraid to believe him," I admit. "I'm even afraid of believing I can change. I don't think I can. I think I'm stuck like this."

"You know what Niimi would say to that?" he asks.

"Yeah, I just gotta let that superhero inside of me wake up," I say.

"That's right. Like your dad did."

"My dad? A superhero?" I laugh. "No way."

"I'll let you in on a little secret . . . In life, we go through three stages. The person-that-needs-help stage, the villain stage, and the superhero stage . . . You get to choose the order. You decide which mask to wear."

This is like his daughter's mission statement she made me write down. They are so similar. Natural born healers.

"You remember your dad as the villain. Then he asked for help. I helped him. Together, we fought the villain inside of him. And now he chooses to be a superhero, for his family . . . For you," he says.

"Not for me. He left me."

"But he also brought you back here, when you needed help to slay your villain."

Are my dad and I really that alike? I accept I was quite the villain. Now, whether I want to admit it or not, I need help . . . That only leaves one more stage for me.

"Maybe you need to spend some more time outside.

Under the family tree. I believe there may be some bottled-up things you need to see," he says and stands.

I take my cue and head back outside, toward the tree in full bloom. As I reach the door, I see him remove his robe. Under it, he wears a nice vintage brown velvet suit. He walks to his meal, at the table, beside two lit candles. He looks out the window, toward the moon, glowing for him. "Sorry I'm late, my love. I had to save the world again," he says, and takes a seat.

He looks at the moon the way my dad looks at Wendy. I guess not even death can keep Niimi's parents apart.

I approach the tree and run my finger over bottle after bottle. I see so many names of people I will probably never meet. So many strangers looking for a light at the end of a dark tunnel. When I close my eyes, I can almost hear their voices. Maybe it's my mind doing this, or maybe this tree is sacred or maybe this is how messages in bottles work. I don't know.

But one thing I do know is that the hope I feel all around me is real. The hope to be helped and healed. I open my eyes and glide my hands over the bottles like an eel gliding over coral reefs. What am I looking for? What does the chief want me to see? Then I stop. A green bottle dangles in front of my face. The name on it is Wendy.

Is this my Wendy?

I grab the bottle and tip it upside down, allowing the small note to slip out the neck and land in my palm. I unfold it and read it. *I am still afraid to drive. But I will try. Also, I don't think Benny likes me. But I will try to connect with him again tomorrow. Bear with me.*

I fold the note and stuff it back into the bottle. Of course Wendy is afraid to drive. Her husband was killed in a car accident. And I made fun of her. She must have been terrified driving me to the bookstore. No wonder she was driving so slowly . . . And she cares whether I like her or not? I guess I can see why she thinks I don't like her. I've gone out of my way to hurt her feelings.

Many times.

But the truth is, I actually do like Wendy. As much as I don't want to, I realize she's pretty awesome.

I see George's bottle. Wendy must have made him one. I open it and read it. I see Lulu's. Oh Gawd, she was asking for help and I stole from her. I'm awful. I read her note too. I see Hank's bottle. Ugh. I stole from him too. I see Alex's. I read them both. Then I see my dad's bottle. I don't need to open his. I know what it says. It helped him get sober. He really did ask for help. He did his boot camp.

And beside his bottle is mine.

My dad made me a bottle. Niimi answered it. She has been trying to bloom me, and I've fought against it the entire time. I've mocked her. I've called her names. I've even accused her of being a fake. I'm such a butthead.

I see why she says I have a hole in my heart. All my actions since I've come to this place have been heartless.

234

I don't need to look inside my bottle either. I know what I need to do.

As I turn to leave, another bottle catches my eye. A bottle hanging at the edge of the tree, away from the rest of them. It's a red bottle with Niimi's name on it.

I grab the bottle and hold it, not sure if I should read the note inside. Even though I've read the others, Niimi's feels too personal to read, like I'm reading from her diary. I release the bottle and watch it sway back and forth.

"I may be wearing a mask, but I have nothing to hide."

I turn around and see Niimi standing there, under the tree.

The way the moonlight passes through all the hanging bottles makes me feel like she's an action hero on a stage, disguised in her mask and reflecting every color from every bottle across her body.

And even though I don't know exactly what she looks like behind the mask, in this moment, it doesn't matter. She is the most beautiful person I have ever seen. "Niimi, I wasn't going to read it," I say.

"It's okay. I want you to," she says.

"You do?"

"You may be leaving tomorrow. You might as well get the answer to that burning question of yours," she says.

"Why you wear the mask," I say.

"Read it aloud," she adds as she catches the swaying bottle and pulls the note out and hands it to me.

I look down at the piece of paper. "Out loud?"

"Loud enough for my mom to hear," she says, and points up at the moon.

I unfold it and clear my throat. "Dad, I tried to take it off today. I really did. But then her smell left me and I panicked. I don't know how to let go of her. I miss her so much. It makes me feel close to her, but you're right. She wouldn't want me to keep wearing it. I need to find the courage to take it off, for good. I'm just not there yet. Bear with me."

That's the end of the note. I fold it and put it back in the bottle. My eyes drift back to Niimi's, which are now glistening.

"She wore it every day for the last year of her life. Her illness attacked her skin. She said it ate away her beauty, but she was still beautiful to me," she says.

"I'm so sorry, Niimi."

"I guess, over time, I just got used to seeing her in this mask. And when she left this world, wearing it was my way of holding on to her. She was my superhero."

All the awful things I've said. I wish I could take them all back. I wish "I'm sorry" wasn't such a two-word throwaway line people say to each other when one is sad. I wish there was something better to say . . . But I have no idea what that would be.

"Has your dad seen this message?" I ask.

"People come and update their bottles as they move along their journeys. We're all works in progress. I came out

here to leave my dad a new message. I guess you can read this one too," she says, and hands me a folded piece of paper.

I unfold it and read it aloud. "Dad, I think I failed with Benny. I need your help with this one. He's stubborn, rude, untrustworthy, and highly uncooperative. But there's also a really sweet boy buried under all that." I immediately tear the strip of paper in half.

"Why would you do something like that?" she asks.

"Because, Niimi . . . You were right about everything you said about me, but you did get one thing wrong."

"And what's that?"

"You didn't fail with me. I am just a very stubborn, rude, untrustworthy, and highly uncooperative work in progress," I say, smiling.

She's silent. Then she smiles.

"Something I said made you smile?" I ask.

"Maybe. You're smiling too."

"I'm smiling because I realized something just now," I say.

"And that is?"

"My body is a world. In that world there are three warriors. A superhero, someone who needs help, and a villain. But there can only be one leader of my world. I've been listening to the villain for a long time. I'm ready to shut him up and listen to the other guy, but I need your help," I say.

Her eyes glisten. "You memorized it, kinda," she says.

"Yeah. I think I know what I need to do now. But I can't do it alone," I say.

"You want me to convince your dad and Wendy that you've changed so you don't have to go back home and face the judge?" she says.

"That's why I came here . . . But there's something else now."

"You want to be a superhero?" she says, with sparks of excitement behind each word.

"I don't need to be a superhero. At least not yet. I just don't want to be a villain anymore."

"Well then, Benny. What do you need?" she asks.

"Directions to Lulu's house and Hank's house," I say. "And I need to borrow your bike."

Niimi pulls out her notepad and writes down the directions, then stuffs them into my pocket.

"Your fight has begun. Remember, fear is a coward," she says, and points to her bike, which is waiting for me near the front door. "Good luck."

CHAPTER 20

MIIGAAZO DIBIKAD [FIGHT NIGHT]

Back in Duluth, my mom never lets me ride my bike alone this late at night. She'd flip out if she knew I were doing it now. But I'm on a mission. And after thirty minutes of riding through the blistering cold, I finally reach Lulu's house. I hop off the bike and approach the front door. But before I knock, fear grips my chest. I know she's going to be pissed. She'll probably punch me in the nose, for real this time.

Maybe I can just leave the mic on the doorstep? She'll get it back, and isn't that the point?

No! I need to come clean. I never should have taken it in the first place. Lulu was cool to me, and I stole from her. She deserves the truth. But as I raise my fist to knock, I see my shadow. It's standing exactly where it should be;

still, something about it is off . . . It's moving . . . but I'm not. What the heck? Goose bumps run up and down my spine, causing my whole body to shiver.

You're not starting to believe in this be-a-good-person crap, are you, Benny? a voice asks.

Was that my voice? It sounded like me. But I didn't speak. "Who said that?" I ask, and look all around me . . . No one is there. Then it hits me . . . It's my freaking shadow, and it is speaking to me. This voice is the villain inside my head.

Let's just keep it and sell it. We're leaving tomorrow anyway.

"I need to do this," I say.

They all think you're a loser, Benny . . . But I don't. I'll never leave you.

"SHUT UP!" I shout. "You're just trying to scare me." And what did Niimi say about fear? Fear is a coward. I just need to confront it.

I take a step forward, toward my shadow. It grows bigger, but I refuse to be afraid, "I'm not listening to you anymore."

Suddenly the porch light shines on. Now my shadow is just a regular shadow. The voice is gone. That was intense. Lulu opens her front door. "Is someone out there?" she asks.

"It's me . . . Benny."

"Benny? What are you doing here?"

"I have something for you," I say.

"Who is it, Lu?" a voice shouts from inside.

"Just some . . . kid I know," she shouts back.

She turns back to me. "Come in. It's freezing out," Lulu says to me.

A few steps in, and I see her apartment hasn't changed. There are still rows of seats, each filled with a stuffed animal, but there's also a human in the front row. I immediately wonder if this person was a stuffed animal moments ago.

"Benny, this is Dessa," she says to me. "Dessa, this is that kid I was telling you about," Lulu says to her.

"The kid that nicked you the shirt?" Dessa asks.

"That's me," I say.

Dessa is just as punk-rock-looking as Lulu, maybe more so. Her torn-up shirt hangs off her shoulders, exposing her dark skin, which glistens as she moves. Oh, that's glitter. A nose ring sparkles atop her left nostril and her hair is shaved on one side, and the side with hair is slicked back in tight black rows. She may be the coolest-looking person I have ever seen.

"Why is he looking at me like that?" Dessa asks.

"Don't worry about it—he was crushing on me too," Lulu says.

I snap out of my daze, "Sorry. I . . ."

"Have something to give me?" Lulu reminds me.

"Yes. I do," I say.

Ugh. It will be a proper beatdown. Two against one. The punk rockers versus the thief. They are both going to attack me the moment I do what I got to do . . . But I got to do it . . . So, here it goes. I'm doing it.

I reach into my backpack and pull out the microphone. Lulu's eyes widen. Dessa stands up. Wow, she's tall. Long legs to kick me with.

"I stole this from you," I say, and extend it to Lulu.

Her eyes narrow in on me. "Why?"

"Because when I met you, it's what I did . . . But now I want to be a bad boy but a good person. Like you said. I'm sorry for stealing it," I say, and close my eyes, waiting for the punch. But . . . it doesn't come.

I open my eyes. Lulu is just staring at the microphone. Her eyes are welled up, about to break. Her hand reaches up and takes it from me. "This was from my mother. It took her three paychecks to afford it. I was so afraid of losing it that I keep it behind glass," she says, beginning to cry.

Dessa approaches her and wraps her arms around Lulu. "Her mother stopped speaking to her two years ago," Dessa says to me.

"Why?" I ask.

"She hasn't accepted who her daughter is," Dessa says.

"Yet . . . But she will," Lulu adds.

"I . . ." There's nothing I can say right now. I can't imagine not speaking to my mom for two years. How sad. "If you want to punch me, I'd understand," I say.

Lulu wipes her tears away. "Punch you?" she says, and wraps her arms around me. "Thank you," she cries while squeezing me tightly.

Wait. Did she seriously just thank me? This place has

taught me how unpredictable some people can be. Maybe she isn't mad at me because, in the end, her microphone is now back where it belongs, in her hands. "How's the singing going?"

"It's getting there. Little by little."

"Baby steps," Dessa says. "She almost got a whole verse out in front of our neighbor this afternoon."

"Then I froze. I tried to picture him as a cow. I asked him to moo. It was awkward," Lulu says.

"We're works in progress," I say, and feel something I don't remember ever feeling before. What is this? It's warm. It feels right. Is this what giving feels like?

I look around the crowd and stare at all the stuffed animal faces. I know Lulu saw them move. Even if it can't be explained, I know it was real. Just like the wolf with Alex. Just like the bear with me. Some things don't have to make sense. I've learned that. I walk toward the front door. "I hope I see you again someday, Lulu."

"Well, if you don't see me, you'll definitely hear me," Lulu says, and smiles.

Lulu looks so happy holding her microphone in one hand and Dessa's hand in the other. Her smile. Her wild eyes. Does it feel like this every time you do something good? No wonder people want to help people. This feels amazing.

"I know I will," I say, and walk out of Lulu's home.

I race down the steps and reach Niimi's bike. This is a new kind of adrenaline. I like it.

But this good feeling is suddenly eclipsed by another new feeling. It must be so hard to do this every single day for so many people while you're dealing with your own life. How does Niimi keep it all together? She inherited the role to bloom the people of Grand Portage. But doesn't she want to do kid stuff too? Doesn't she want to hang out with friends? What if she just wants to goof around and go to the movies or ice skating? Shouldn't she be back in school with everyone else her age? Has anyone asked her what she wants? It must be so heavy. All that pressure. All that responsibility. All of that while missing her mom.

A cold breeze swoops down and sends chills throughout my body, reminding me I need to get moving. I don't have much time left.

I hop onto Niimi's bike and pull out the directions to Hank's house. As I read them, another breeze passes through me, standing up all the tiny hairs on the back of my neck. It wasn't just chilled breeze, there was a bit of fear mixed in there. Hank is a hunter. Hank has a gun. I stole from him.

I ride toward his house, but with each pedal, I'm not thinking about Hank or his gun, or Wendy and her missing necklace, or my mom or dad or George . . . I'm thinking about Niimi again. And not because I want her to save my butt by telling everyone I'm blooming, but I'm thinking about her because after tomorrow, I'm no longer going to be around her, and that sends a strange pain into my gut.

And even though I can be quite difficult, I like who I am when I'm around her, or at least, I like who I am becoming. But that's not just it. The truth is, I like her. She's funny and strange and tries so hard to make everyone around her feel better. But after tomorrow, she'll be here, and I'll probably be back in Duluth.

A half hour later, I finally reach Hank's house. I am pretty much an ice pop now. I don't know how I'm going to make it home being this cold, but I'll worry about that after I give this compass back.

His house is run-down and small. The shell of a rusted car with no interior sits in the front yard. Two large, tattered American flags protrude from the porch roof. The grass is dead, yellow, and covered in car parts. I'm starting to think this car may have exploded right here on the lawn.

I climb off the bike and lean it against the gate in front of the house.

I approach the front door. Here goes everything. But before I knock, I see movement from within the house through the window. I peer over to it, to get a better look. Inside, I see Hank and his son, Alex, playing in the living room. Alex wears a red towel like a cape and stands on the couch, shouting down to his father, who is sitting on the carpet, wearing a small trash can on his head. I can't hear what Alex is saying, but he's holding an aluminum foil sword high into the air and is laughing in between each of his words.

When Hank growls and lifts his arms like a monster, Alex leaps off the couch and lands on his father, tackling him. Together, they both roll around the carpet as Alex slices and dices his trash-can-monster-dad's chest and belly. And even though I can't hear their words to each other, their laughter sneaks under the window frame and travels out to me. It's a laughter I once had with my dad. Father and son time. That was my favorite part of my day. A part of me wants to hop through the window and join in on the monster slaying, but this is Alex's time. He's worked hard for it. He just got his father back.

My mom was a pretty good monster to tackle in my dad's absence. She tried really hard to be two parents at once. The fun one and the strict one. The cook and the playmate. The one to tuck me in and the one to wake me up. Wow. My mom did it all on her own. That sounds like a superpower to me. And how did I thank her? I went out and got into trouble, no matter how hard she tried to steer me clear from it. I refused to listen. And she even sent me here, as a last shot to straighten me out. I can't screw this up. I owe it to my mom to be the best version of myself.

I knock on the door, and two seconds later I hear a child's feet shuffling through the house to the door. I take a deep breath and try not to think of Hank as a hunter, but Hank as a fun trash-can-head monster dad instead. "People change," I whisper to myself as the door opens.

Alex sees me and smiles. "Benny!"

"It's me. Can I talk to your dad really quick?" I ask.

"Dad!" Alex shouts.

Hank approaches and stands behind his son, towering over him at the doorway. "Did she send you to check up on us already?" Hank asks. "We're doing just fine."

That would be an easy out. I could say yes and leave, but I'm done looking for the easy way out. "No. I came here to give you something," I say.

"Okay, come in. You'll freeze your toes off out here," he says, and widens the door enough for me to enter.

"I can't stay. It's late, and I am leaving tomorrow, but before I go, I need to do this," I say.

"Do what?"

I reach into my backpack and pull out his compass. His eyes focus on it, but slowly rise to meet mine.

"Isn't that grandpa's compass, Dad?" Alex says.

"It is," he tells his son. "How do you have it?"

"I stole it from you," I say.

Hank's eyes narrow in on me. He rubs his chin. I bet he's thinking about knocking my lights out, but hopefully he won't, not with his kid watching. "Why?" he asks.

There's no reason why I steal from people. No good reason, at least. "I don't know why. Maybe because..."

"Maybe because he was lost, Daddy. He needed it. But now he found his way home, and he's here to give it back, right?" Alex says to his father.

"Yeah, Alex. You're so smart. I think he was lost. Looks

like he and I both found our way back home," Hank says, and takes the compass from my hand.

Thanks, kid. You may have just saved my nose from a lot of pain.

"Alex, why don't you start setting up that fort we talked about. I'm just going to say bye to our friend here, okay?"

"Okay. Bye," Alex says to me.

"Oh Alex, before you go, I have something for you too," I say, and pull the stuffed bear out of my backpack. "This guy needs a home."

Alex takes the stuffed bear and hugs me. I don't think I've ever been hugged by a kid before. They are bony little creatures.

As Alex runs off with his bear, Hank takes a step toward me. Oh, no. Here's comes the punch. Here comes the head-lock. The choke hold. I close my eyes and pray he does it quick . . . But just like the slug to the nose by Lulu that never came, neither does this one. Instead, I open my eyes and see he is holding out his hand to me. Seriously?

I nervously extend mine, and we shake hands. His grip is strong. He could easily crush my fingers if he wanted to . . . But he doesn't. He is smiling. "Second chances. They're life-savers, aren't they?" he says.

"Yes. They really are," I say.

"Take care, kid," Hank says, and releases my hand.

He closes the door and goes back to playing with his son.

Another warm feeling fills my body. It's not the rush of blood that stealing used to give me or the happy feeling that giving now gives me. It's a different one. It's a calmness inside of me that makes my entire body smile. This is what being given a second chance feels like.

CHAPTER 21

AKAWE OJIIM [FIRST KISS]

I slept with all three dogs piled onto me, and I'll admit, although I now smell like dog, they kept me incredibly warm through the night. I might be leaving today. It's strange. Last night began with me trying to do something good so I wouldn't be sent back to the judge, but after seeing the bottle tree in full bloom, I stopped caring what was going to happen to me, and it became all about what I could do for Lulu, Hank, Alex, and Niimi. I don't necessarily feel like I'm turning into a superhero or anything. I don't feel physically different. I feel like I just returned a few stolen items. That's all. That doesn't make me good; it just makes me less bad. But being less bad is a good start, right?

After I get dressed, I sit on the bed and think about the stuffed bear that started all of this. I still don't know our connection. My dad asked if I remembered it. I don't. So many parts of my childhood are behind locked doors, buried somewhere deep inside of me. I hope Niimi comes to tell my dad and Wendy what I did last night. Even if it doesn't save me from the judge, I'd still like them to know that somehow my trip to Grand Portage helped me. Because it did. I don't want to steal from people anymore. Life is hard enough, and the last thing anyone needs is some punk taking things from them. I now realize what Wendy meant when she said every time I steal from someone, I steal from everyone. Because trust gets stolen. And without trust, we really do have nothing.

My dad opens the door and enters. I guess he came to wake me up and make sure I'm ready to go to the bus station. "Hey, Benny. How was your sleep?" he asks.

"I dreamt I was wrestling three smelly dogs over the blanket all night. Oh, wait, that really happened," I say.

He laughs. "They like you. They don't just cuddle with anyone, ya know."

Small talk, okay, so he is nervous too. "I know you think I let you down, Dad, but before I leave today, I hope you'll see I have changed, at least a little bit," I say.

"We let each other down, Benny. I guess you and I have more in common than you'd like to admit, huh?" he asks.

He sits down beside me. I know he thinks I am a thief and all I did while I was here was steal from people, and he's partly right, but something inside of me wants to tell him I am so much more than that now. I want to tell him that for the first time in seven years, I feel good.

"Everyone tells me you're this great guy now," I say. "But I have no idea who I am."

He smiles. "That's called being human. We'll spend our whole lives trying to figure out who we are. No one gets it right. No one's perfect. These things take time. No one becomes a strong oak overnight. But you got to plant the seed to one day get there. The trick is to take it day by day. And hey, whoever you choose to be, you are stuck with you. Might as well be someone you like being around," he says and places his hand on my knee.

"That's gonna be hard. I've heard I'm a pain in the neck."

He chuckles and removes his hand. "Speaking of necks, Wendy would really appreciate getting her necklace back. She's pretty distraught about it."

There's no use telling him I didn't take it. I already have many times. "Did you talk to Niimi this morning?" I ask.

"No. But her father called last night. We had a good talk."

Suddenly, a car door shuts rights outside the house. I hear Niimi shout goodbye to her father and a car drive off. Yes! She came!

Niimi enters the garage.

My dad stands up. "We're going in a half hour. I'll leave you two alone for a bit," he says, and leaves the garage. If she's here, she must not think of me as completely hopeless.

re is some good hiding somewhere

d she sees it—even if no one else

her I faced my villain. I told it to

now that doesn't make me a super-

at means I am no longer the villain.

puffy red jacket, jeans, and a pink

ver her mask. She looks so cute. She

he enters, revealing a black thermal

-painted handprint on it. "Mino-

nean?" I ask.

he replies.

ood days are way better than bad days.

m leaving or good because I am stay-

d because it's nice outside," she says.

need to remember that not everything

, I'm still learning.

ned the microphone and the compass

llence. I know I should be thinking of

I am staying or going, or about Wendy's

ut how absolutely strange the past few days

But I find myself only thinking about one

irl in front of me.

"I'm not here to save your butt. Only you can d
now. And I'm not here to say goodbye either," she say

"Then why are you here?" I ask.

"Because, Benny, even though it makes no sens
even though you are incredibly frustrating and bullhe
I am here to just do this."

"Look at me?"

"Yeah. Look at you. Talk to you. Just this."

Something swirls inside of my stomach. Happy s
Nervous swirls. Aren't they supposed to feel like butter
They feel more like grizzlies. My hands begin to sweat
knees begin to go weak. What is this feeling? And wh
I smiling like this? It feels like both corners of my lip
about to touch my ears. Ugh. I'm blushing. The same
my mom did when she was staring at that average-loo
judge. "I like . . . this too," I say.

Niimi takes a step toward me. "I wish you could
met my mom. She would have liked you. She always ro
for the underdog."

This is the first time she's brought her mom up with
I know it's probably really hard to talk about, but Ni
is so strong. She's trying. And then last night's words f
back to me . . . We are all works in progress. Even su
heroes like her.

"Maybe one day you can tell me all about her," I say,
take a step closer to her.

Her eyes smile and invite me to take another step. She has such beautiful eyes.

"Remember the day we first met, you told me that I need to wake up the superhero inside of me?"

"I remember. You laughed at me," she says.

"I didn't believe in it then. But I've seen it wake up in people. And I've seen their superpowers come alive. You helped Lulu become a super-singer. Her power is she moves people with her voice. You helped Hank become a super-dad. His power is he can put down his gun and pick up his son. You helped Alex become a super-son. His power is giving grown men like his dad their childhoods back. But you. You're the best superhero of them all, because your superpower is seeing the potential in people that no one else can see. Like in me. You see me behind the mask I wear."

She's silent. I see tears form under her eyes, like two tiny lakes that are about to become two rivers. "Superheroes are everywhere, if you look for them. They put out our fires. They heal our bones. They teach us how to ride a bike. They teach us math and spelling. They help old ladies across the street. They feed stray cats and make sure you don't go to bed hungry," she says.

"They're everywhere. Even in our books and movies and songs, constantly reminding us that they're real. You were right, Niimi. About everything. Thank you for not giving up on me, Niimi."

"I'm not a quitter. Maybe I'm just as stubborn as you are," she says.

We stare at each other. Neither of us says a word. And for a moment, I completely forget that she's even wearing a mask. And she's the most beautiful person I have ever seen.

Then a strange thought pops into my head. A thought I have never had before. I want to kiss her. What should I do? Should I kiss her? But I'm so nervous. We just stare into each other's eyes, each waiting for the other to say something.

"I've never wanted to kiss anybody before," I say.

She laughs. Oh great. She's laughing. Is she laughing at me or with me? I laugh. Crap. Now I'm laughing. Am I laughing at me or with her?

"What do we do now?" I ask.

"We can shut up," she says.

I smile. Shutting up means no more talking. No more talking means . . . we should kiss?

I take one last step toward her, but my foot kicks over an empty glass bottle. I was so thirsty and tired last night that I took it from the fridge when I got home and drank it in bed. It rolls across the room. We both stare at it. I bet we're both thinking of the same thing: the tree full of bottled-up messages.

That's it!

"That's what?" she asks.

"I'm not here to magically become a better person. My dad isn't perfect now. Wendy isn't perfect. You're not perfect. No one is. I'm here to start boot camp, that's it. But boot camp lasts forever. Life is our boot camp. We just need to stay stubborn and never give up, even when it's hard." I'm so excited, I can barely catch my breath.

"My mom used to say all people should come with a warning label tattooed on them that says *still learning, bear with me*," she says.

Bear with me. Each bottle I opened had a message that ended with those three words. *Bear with me.* Like the bear that I encountered in the forest. Like the stuffed bear. The reason why I'm here. All of this has happened because of that bear . . . And for the first time, I finally know why I freeze every time I see it. I hated that stuffed bear. I was afraid of it. But the superhero inside of me is waking up, and with it, one of my buried memories has resurfaced. I remember the stuffed bear now.

It was early in the morning, the day my father left us. He entered my room to say goodbye. I was so angry. I refused to talk to him. I didn't want him to leave. I didn't want him to explain why he was going. But before he did, he placed a stuffed bear on my bed with a note that said *I'm sorry. I'm getting help. Bear with me.*

As soon as he left my room, I tore up his message and threw the bear away. I didn't want to bear with him. I wanted to be with him. And the next time I saw that bear was seven years later in the department store. I didn't recognize it, but something inside of me told me I had to take it.

I don't hate the bear. I love it.

I snap out of my memory and look into Niimi's eyes. "My dad once told me that hurt people hurt people, and that's why I've been stealing. Because I was in pain ... But you have shown me that helped people help people. And now that's what I need to do."

"You better be careful—you're sounding an awful lot like a superhero," she says.

I pick up the bottle and approach her. "I need string and a staple gun."

"Before you get the string, you need a name," she says.

I smile. "The Thief sounds a little too much like a villain, doesn't it?"

"I was thinking ... How about ... 'Benny the Bear'?"

"I like it. The Bear and She Is Dancing, There Is Lightning. We sound pretty heroic," I say and grab one of the stepladders leaning against the wall.

"I'll get the stuff from your dad's office," she says, and leaves the garage.

I follow her out, and while she heads down the hall, I stop in the middle of the living room. I set the stepladder and wait for Niimi. When she returns with the staple gun and string, I climb to the highest step and staple one end of the string to the ceiling, letting the other end hang down. Then I tie the neck of the bottle to the string. With Niimi's Sharpie, I write *George* across the bottle. If I can't bring him to the message tree, then I'll bring the message tree to him.

My dad and Wendy enter the house with the three dogs. When they see the bottle hanging down in the center of the living room, they stop.

"What's going on?" Wendy asks.

"If you wanted to leave me a message, you could have just told me in the Jeep," my dad says.

"It's not for you. It's for George," Niimi says.

Wendy smiles. "Was this your idea?"

"No. It was his," Niimi says, and points to me.

"You ready to give Wendy her necklace back?" my dad asks.

"Nope," I say.

"Then . . . you ready to go home?" he adds.

"Not yet," I say, and I knock on George's door.

George opens it. "You're still here?"

"Yeah. I want you to see something," I say, and walk toward the living room.

George follows me in. He sees the bottle hanging. He sees his name on it. He looks at me with confused eyes. "Please don't tell me this is some creepy mistletoe kind of thing."

"No. This is for you. You put a message inside. Anything you want help with. Could be something small like needing

259

a pep talk to get you driving again," I say, and look at Wendy. "It could be something big like asking for help to turn your life around." I look at my dad. "Or it could even be something huge like asking for help to remind you who you were before your dad died," I say, and look at George. "The point is, if you leave a message in this bottle, there will be someone here to answer it."

George stares at me. He's so hard to read. I can't tell if he wants to punch me or hug me. "Thanks" is all he says, and walks back toward his room.

But I'm okay with that. He didn't yell. He didn't yank it down and crack it over my head. He didn't even make fun of it. I'm not going to tell him to snap out of it or tell him there's nothing to be afraid of, because that will only make him angry. I should know; it made me angry every time I was told that. All I can do is do what Niimi did for me. Let him know people are here for him. Let him know he's not alone. Whether he knows it or not, George's boot camp just started. He has a long way to go, but like my dad says, no one becomes a strong oak overnight.

"I am ready now," I say, and look at my dad and Wendy.

My dad nods. Wendy sighs.

"Wait," George says from behind me.

I watch him walk out of his room, and back into the living room . . . and in his hand is Wendy's necklace.

"George?" Wendy says.

"I took it so you'd all blame him and make him leave,"

George says to his mother, whose mouth is open in surprise. I guess we are all surprised.

"I don't know how you do it, dude. Stealing. I felt like crap the entire time. And I figure, you got enough problems, you don't need me adding one more," he says, and hands me the necklace. "Sorry."

I turn around and hand it to Wendy. She's speechless. I turn back to George.

"This doesn't mean we're friends or anything like that, I still think you're ugly and smell bad," he says to me, half smiling.

"Thanks, George. I like you too," I say.

"And I'm not saying I'm ever going to use this thing," he says, pointing to the bottle hanging in the center of the living room. "But . . . we can keep it hanging here for a while. I guess." He gives the dangling bottle a small tap. "Bye, Benny," he says, and retreats back into his bedroom.

That's the first time he's ever called me by my name. Wow. He's taking steps forward already. Baby steps, but baby steps are still steps. And that's all that matters.

"I owe you an apology," Wendy says to me.

I turn to face her. "No, you don't. I broke the rules. I stole while I was here, and like you said when we met, if I steal from anyone, I steal from you," I say.

"I did say that, didn't I?"

"Yeah. I'm just glad you didn't drag me out and bury me in the woods." I turn to my dad. "We should get going."

He looks confused. "I don't see what the rush is. Maybe you can stay for a few more days. Seeing that Wendy got the necklace back," he says.

"I do want to stay, but I think I owe it to my mom to be there for her. She needs to know she got her son back. I think she and I need to get to know each other again," I say.

"I think she'd love that," he says.

Then my eyes turn to Niimi. She is the hardest part about wanting to go back home.

"Come on, Tommy. You can drop me off at the shop. Let's give them some time to say goodbye," Wendy says to my dad.

"Zaagaandaa!" he shouts, and all three watch dogs race outside with him and Wendy.

I turn to Niimi. This is so hard. I know I'll see her again. I'll try to come up on weekends and school breaks, but I also know how busy Niimi is. The world has no shortage of people who need her help.

CHAPTER 22

NIIZH AANDEGWAG (TWO CROWS)

Niimi stares at me with eyes that are happy and sad at the same time. "What you said to George, that was really nice."

"Well, I have a pretty good teacher," I say, and approach her, getting as close to her as I was in the garage.

"I guess my job here is done. I should get going," she says.

"Wait." Before I know it, I've taken her hand. "Everything inside of me is telling me to stay, just so I can be with you. But being here has also shown me how hard my mom has tried, and now I need to show her all the hard work paid off. I need to make her proud of me again, and the truth is, I actually miss her. Is that strange?" I ask.

"Not strange at all. I miss my mom every day. But mine

is life and death away. Yours is only one hundred and forty-five miles away. You should go . . . But you should also come back," she says.

"I'd love to. If you're not too busy blooming people," I say.

"Well . . . After you talked to my dad last night, I guess it reminded him of what kids need. He spoke to my mom in his dream, and they both decided they aren't quite ready for me to grow up just yet."

"What does that mean?" I ask.

"It means my dad is going to train someone else to handle the blooming while he remains focused on everything else. It means I'm going back to school," she says with a burst of joy in her voice.

"So, we can hang out on the weekends?" I say, matching her level of joy.

"Yeah. That's exactly what it means. But before you go . . . I'm going to need my bike back," she says.

"It's in the garage. Thanks for letting me borrow it," I say, and lead her to the garage.

But as we enter it and head toward where I left it—it's gone.

"Where is it?" she asks.

"I . . . left it right here," I say, and approach the spot.

Instead of her bike, there's a Post-it note from my dad. It reads *Her bike is in the Jeep. We're waiting outside.*

Niimi follows me outside. Wendy and my dad are waiting

for us in the Jeep. "We'll drop you off at home, but we got to make a quick stop first," my dad says to Niimi.

"Out," he shouts, and all three dogs leap out the back seat and take to the field.

Niimi and I climb inside the back of the Jeep. I smile when I realize it is Wendy who is behind the wheel.

"Buckle up, buckaroos," Wendy says.

We drive down the road and enter the familiar highway. The wind whips my hair as I stare out toward Lake Superior. I feel happy. I slide my hand into Niimi's hand, and together we both move our fingers across each other's skin like we are massaging a baby bird.

We aren't heading to Niimi's house or the bus station, and instead we pull into the parking lot of Wendy's bookstore.

"What are we doing here?" I ask.

"We're dropping Wendy off, and there's something I need to grab," my dad says, and he exits the Jeep.

Wendy gets out and heads toward the front door of her bookshop. Niimi and I hop out to join them. "Back to the scene of the crime," Niimi says as we enter.

And the boring bookstore I dreaded being in when I arrived in Grand Portage now has a totally different feel to it. Maybe Benny the Thief didn't like books, but that doesn't mean Benny the Bear doesn't. Who knows, maybe I'll see what all the fuss is about. I've never actually read a book before; in school I read only the beginnings and ends. And the way Niimi twirls and sniffs the books tells me that there must be something to love about places like this.

My dad and Wendy head to the back, leaving Niimi and me alone.

"I remember how miserable you were in this place," she says to me.

"Yeah. You ruined that for me," I say.

"Ruined it? How so?"

"I can never be miserable in a bookstore again. Because it was in a bookstore where we first met," I say.

"But I don't want you to just not be miserable in a bookstore; I want you to love bookstores," she says as she approaches me and runs her finger along the spines of the books near us.

"How would you make me love bookstores?" I ask, noticing I'm getting more nervous the closer she gets to me.

"Well . . . the only thing better than having this place be where we first met is for it to be the place where we had our first kiss," she says.

My heart immediately beats faster. My palms sweat. Did she really just say that? My knees feel weak. And my cheeks hurt from smiling so much.

"I do think that would make me love bookstores," I say, tripping over my words.

She takes a deep breath and reaches a hand to her mask. "Close your eyes," she says.

I close them. Is she removing her mask? I honestly forgot

she was even wearing one. I don't care what she looks like. I just want to—

"Okay, open them," she says.

I slowly open my eyes. I see her feet. Red Chucks. My eyes rise a bit higher. Denim jeans slightly faded. One of those belts that look like a seat belt. Cute. Her hips peek out from under her shirt. It's a black shirt. Long sleeves. My eyes rise even higher. I swallow. I'm so nervous. I see her neck. It's thin, reminds me of a bird, I don't know why. Black hair. Long. Two braids. I see her chin. A freckle. I see her mouth. She's smiling. Lips are shining. Red. As always. White teeth. So white. A little crooked, but in a good way. She has dimples. I don't know how to kiss. I see her nose. I see her eyes. Large. Round. Brown. Wild. My heart's beating so fast. I see her entire face. And even though most of her face has been hidden since we've met, she looks exactly as I imagined. Mask or no mask. I can't pull my eyes off her. She is dancing, there is lightning.

"Life is a trip, isn't it?"

"It's a boot camp," I reply.

She smiles. I smile back. We stare at each other, not as superheroes, but as boy and girl. As friends. As something more than friends.

I offer her my hand. She takes it. Our fingers intertwine like runaway vines. Our palms begin to sweat together. She's nervous too. She pulls me closer as I pull her closer. Our bodies touch. I wonder if she can hear the marching band in my chest. Then our eyes close and . . . we kiss.

This is my first kiss. And it's so real. Not like the fake kisses you see in movies. Or the kind teenagers brag about. They got it all wrong. This kiss is the first of its kind. There's never been a kiss like this. It's a superhero kiss.

Our faces separate. I still taste her on my lips. She smells like wild strawberries.

WAIT! Is this how my dad feels about Wendy? Is this how Wendy feels about food? I reach up and touch Niimi's face, to make sure she's real. To make sure I'm not dreaming. I remember the first time I saw her here. She walked into my life like she was dancing. I didn't know it then, but that was the moment lightning struck. And it's been striking me ever since.

"She Is Dancing. There Is Lightning." I say her name.

"Benny the Bear. I'm glad I am the last person you stole from," she says.

"I never stole from you," I say.

"But you did," she says and puts my hand over her heart. "From right under my nose."

I smile. I can't believe I love a superhero. I can't believe a superhero loves me.

With one hand, she puts the mask back on. "Baby steps," she says.

"As long as we keep taking 'em, we'll get there. Wherever 'there' is," I say.

"I should get going. I have a lot of schoolwork to catch up on," she says, and walks toward the front door.

I need to say something. Even though she already knows I like her, our last words in person should be memorable.

"Miigwech," I blurt out, remembering one of the first Ojibwe words my parents ever taught me. A very important word. Maybe the most important word . . . thank you.

She smiles. "Giga'waabamin," she replies.

"What's that mean?" I ask.

"Figure it out," she says, and walks out of the store.

I watch her grab her bike out of the Jeep and ride off toward her house.

And the farther she gets from me, the more I feel a heavy pain in my heart. It's not the hole in my heart I had when I first arrived. It's the pain of my heart now being whole. It's the pain of giving my heart to Niimi.

"That's why it's called a crush. Because it hurts," my dad says from behind me.

I turn around and see him and Wendy standing there.

"Were you guys there the whole time?" I ask.

"Us? What? No. We were reading. In the back," Wendy says.

"Yeah, we definitely did not see any kissing," my dad adds.

"None. Whatsoever. But I am thrilled to hear that you love bookstores now," Wendy says.

"You did see everything!" I say.

"Relax. Our first kiss was in this bookstore too. But we were in the next aisle over. The adult section," Wendy says.

"No, it was in the last aisle. You wanted it to be near all the cookbooks," my dad says.

"Oh, yeah. That's right. Now I'm hungry," she says.

I laugh . . . But after I do, the pain returns.

"I've never felt like this before. Does it get easier?"

"Easier? You kidding? It gets harder. But in the best way possible," my dad says.

"I'm going to give you two some time to talk. Benny, this isn't a goodbye hug, it's an I'll-see-you-soon hug. Got it?"

"Got it. And thanks for everything, Wendy," I say.

"And who knows, maybe when you're a bit older, there's a summer job here waiting for you," she says.

"I'd like that. I have a feeling I'll be here every summer."

"I do too," Wendy says as she walks back toward her office.

My dad turns to me. There's so much we need to say to each other . . . But neither of us know how to begin. I guess we are a lot alike, after all. We just stare at each other and nod. But I know the perfect way to get him talking.

"You got a joke? Maybe that will get my mind off her," I ask.

He smiles. "How did the phone propose to his girl-friend?" he asks.

"How?"

"He gave her a ring," he says.

I laugh . . . "I'm going to miss this place."

"This place is going to miss you too."

I smile. He nods. I have a happy dad again. He has a happy son again. It only took seven years to get here, but what can I say? We're slow learners.

"I want you to take this book home with you," he says, and wipes his eye as he walks over toward the back wall and plucks a book from the shelf.

Is he crying? "Which one?" I say, and start walking toward him.

He hands it to me. It's a book on the Ojibwe language. And I don't know how to explain it, but for some reason this book makes me so happy.

"I was hoping we could pick up where we left off. I was teaching you our language when you were young. I'd like to continue that, if you like?"

"I'd like that. Do I need to buy this? Because I don't know if you've heard, but I put my shoplifting days behind me," I say.

He laughs. "I bought it the day your mom called me and asked for help. It's been waiting here for you," he says.

I don't know what to say. We need to say so much more to each other, but that's okay, because now we have time. "We should get going if we want to make the bus."

"I was hoping you'd let me take you home."

"Really? You want to drive me all the way to Duluth?" I ask.

"I do."

I smile. "That's a lot of Beep Beep Jeep. You sure your arm can handle it?"

"Only one way to find out. Let's go," he says, and walks toward the front door.

I carry my book with me as I step outside and walk toward the Jeep.

I take one last look at the bookstore. The scene of the kiss. This place feels like home to me now. Maybe not the home where I'll live most of the time, but my home away from home.

I climb into the passenger side and realize that I just didn't get my dad back, but I pretty much just gained an entire family.

We don't say much on the drive to Duluth. I guess we we're both taking in everything that happened. Maybe we're both afraid if one of us opens our mouths to speak, it will release the dam and we'll spend the entire drive crying. Dad turns on the radio, and it is still on the R&B station. We must listen to fifty love ballads. This time we both laugh.

As we enter Duluth and pull up to my street, he reaches over and puts his hand on my shoulder. "I'm proud of you, Benny."

I don't know why, but those five words nearly erupt me in tears. They are simple words. Nice words. Words that shouldn't make someone cry, but the moment I hear them come out of my dad's mouth, they hit me like those were the five most important words that I'll ever need to hear. He's proud of me. My dad is proud of me. And the truth is, I am proud of him too.

"I forgive you, Dad."

He nods. It's something I thought I'd never say to him, but by his glistening eyes, I can tell it is something he has dreamt of hearing for the last seven years.

As the Jeep idles, he points to two crows sitting together atop a telephone wire. "You know what they call two crows that are always together like that?" he asks. "Velcros."

I laugh. That was one of his better ones. Even he's laughing.

I reach over and hug him, and as I'm in his arms, we both let it out to get it out. Not a loud dramatic cry, but a good cry. A goodbye cry. A cry so many parents and children share on the curbs when being dropped off.

"Give your mother my best," he says after finally releasing me.

"You don't want to come in and say hi?" I ask.

"Baby steps. I'm still a work in progress."

"I get it," I say, wiping my eyes and exiting the Jeep. "Maybe next time I'm up there, we can go see that really old cedar tree?"

He smiles. "I do believe you're ready for that. Oh, and say hi to that handsome judge for me," he says as I pull my suitcase out of the back.

"I don't plan on seeing him again," I say.

My dad laughs. "Oh, you'll be seeing a lot of him."

What! Oh . . . no. It can't be . . .

"What do you mean?" I ask.

"Well, after your court date with him, your mother had her own. Then another one," he says.

"Mom is dating the judge?" I say in disbelief.

"Guilty," he says, laughing.

He reaches under his seat and pulls out something wrapped in newsprint. "This is for you, but don't open it until you're in your room," he says, and hands it to me. "Oh, and before I go, I need to tell you a secret," he says.

Is this the advice that I'll take with me for the rest of my life? Is this wisdom passed down from an Ojibwe father to his son? I lean in and await his words.

He whispers in my ear, "Beep Beep Jeep," and punches me in the shoulder and points to another Jeep parked across the street.

Ouch! As I pull back, he laughs and speeds off.

I smile and rub my shoulder. For a changed man, some things about him haven't changed at all. And I hope they never will.

I walk toward our apartment and it kind of feels like I'm walking on clouds. So much has happened here. I became a superhero. Of course I am going to make mistakes and not be perfect, but I know I won't steal anymore. No matter what that villainous voice in my head says. Those days are behind me. It won't always be easy, but that's okay. Nothing worth anything ever is. But the best part about this trip is . . .

I have a girlfriend now. My mom is going to flip out when I tell her. We've never once talked about girls. And I predict I now won't be able to shut up about her. I can't wait for them to meet one day. Niimi needs a mom in her life. And I have a great one.

I enter my apartment and head toward my room. My mom is still at work. And even though this place is much smaller than my dad's house, it feels so good to be home. I sit on my bed and place my Ojibwe book on my pillow. I look at the present my dad got me. I smile and peel back the corners of the paper and tear it open. I wonder what it is.

It is a ceramic bear, painted to look exactly like the stuffed bear that sent me here. The same bear my dad left for me so many years ago. A note is taped to it: *Thanks for Bearing with me—Dad.*

He made this for me. And I'm in bed, in my room, exactly where I was when I was given the stuffed bear seven years ago. But this time, I'm not tearing up the note and throwing the bear away. Instead, I set it on my bedside table, where it will stand proudly.

CHAPTER 23

SUPERHERO SIGN-UP

I've been back at North Duluth Middle School for one week now. Things are going pretty well. It's still unusual for me to actually attend class, but I'll get used to it. I told all my teachers that I'd like a second chance, and to bear with me, and surprisingly, they all agreed to give me one.

I still get the urge to steal sometimes. It's not like it's going to magically go away overnight, but I've learned to ignore it. I don't want to hurt people anymore. I'd rather do another four-letter word that begins with *H*: I'd rather *help* people. And I'm studying Ojibwe again. Niimi even quizzes me on words. Did you know that the word *help* in Ojibwe is *wiiji*? And the word for *friend* is *niiji*. They rhyme. Pretty cool, huh? My mom says if you ever want to make a niiji, all you got to do is wiiji a stranger. And it's true. Everyone in Grand Portage helped me, and I consider them all my friends now.

My dad gave me an update yesterday. He said that George placed a note in the bottle the other night. I hope he's ready to experience the wildest time of his life. Boot camps up in Grand Portage are no joke. I can't wait to hear about what he goes through. Hopefully, when he defeats his villain and conquers his fear, he can go bike riding with Niimi and me when I'm up there.

I've spoken to Niimi nearly every night. She's basically the only person my age that I talk to, since all of my friends here in Duluth ditched me now that I'm done with stealing. And without friends, I will admit, middle school is a really lonely place . . . So, Niimi gave me a great idea. A brilliant plan to not only make new friends but to also make Duluth a better place. In the library, a place where I've never set foot in before but now go to every day, there is a bulletin post for students to tack flyers onto. Most of them are for study groups, after-school sports, tutoring, or music lessons . . . But what I posted on it is something no school has ever seen before.

DO YOU WANT TO BE A SUPERHERO?
LEAVE YOUR NAME & NUMBER BELOW:

I left room on the sheet for ten names and thought it would be completely full by lunchtime, but when I checked it, only one person had signed up. Someone named *Collin The Brave*.

But you know what they say, if you can reach one person, you can reach a million.

Oh, and my mom and I are closer than ever before . . . She can't wait to meet Niimi. She basically hears about her every single day. She said she brags to her clients at work that her son is dating a superhero. And yes, she's still going out with Judge Mason. His first name is Zachary, but sometimes I still call him the judge. When I do that, he calls me case number 83-212. It's kind of an inside joke we have together. And okay, I'll finally admit it, he is pretty good-looking.

And like Niimi says, giga'waabamin.

If you want to know what that means, I'll tell you what she told me.

Figure it out.

ACKNOWLEDGMENTS

Chi-Miigwech to Robert DesJarlait of Red Lake Ojibwe for walking beside me on this book's journey and helping me with all the Anishinaabemowin. You are a great mentor, artist, and niiji. If you never stop teaching, I will never stop learning.

Miigwech to all of the members of Grand Portage Ojibwe for supporting me and encouraging me to continue my path as a storyteller. I will forever strive to make you proud.

Miigwech to my agent and friend Rosemary Stimola, who loves books more than anyone I have ever known. Thank you for always having my back. Miigwech to my editor and friend Liz Szabla, who makes me a stronger writer, chapter by chapter, book by book. Miigwech to Jean Feiwel and everyone at Feiwel & Friends for continuing to believe in me. Miigwech to everyone at Macmillan for making me a part of your family.

Miigwech to Native artist, Steph Littlebird, for illustrating such a beautiful book cover. Thank you to creative director, Rich Deas, for designing the cover. Thank you to my production editors, Starr Baer and Helen Seachrist, and the production manager, Kim Waymer. And thank you once again, to the associate publicist, Madison Furr.

Miigwech to the wonderful authors in my life who endlessly inspire me and are always rooting for me; Adriana Mather, Nic Stone, Jennifer Niven, Nikita Remi, A.S. King, and Emily Henry.

Miigwech to my dear friends and family for pulling me back down to earth when my head was too busy exploring new unwritten worlds. Miigwech to Sasa, the Hexum family, Tantoo Cardinal, Graham Greene, Michael Greyeyes, Susan James, James Vukelich, all the teachers and librarians, and everyone at FAMB for all your support.

Miigwech to all my fellow Native American authors and artists for continuing to tell our stories so the next generation of readers can learn from our words and create new worlds of their own.

Thank you to my animals, Von, Princess, Tu, and Banana for reminding me every day what happiness is. And to my best friend, Smeagle: travel well, have fun. I love you.

And most importantly, Chi-Miigwech to my beautiful son, Wolf. I wrote this for you. Everything I do is for you. You teach me how to live life every day. I am the man I am because of the man you are. I will never stop dancing with you. I love you.

Thank you for reading this Feiwel & Friends book.
The friends who made *The Second Chance of
Benjamin Waterfalls* possible are:

Jean Feiwel, Publisher
Liz Szabla, Associate Publisher
Rich Deas, Senior Creative Director
Holly West, Senior Editor
Anna Roberto, Senior Editor
Kat Brzozowski, Senior Editor
Dawn Ryan, Executive Managing Editor
Kim Waymer, Senior Production Manager
Erin Siu, Associate Editor
Emily Settle, Associate Editor
Foyinsi Adegbonmire, Associate Editor
Rachel Diebel, Assistant Editor
Angela Jun, Designer
Starr Baer, Associate Copy Chief
Helen Seachrist, Senior Production Editor

Follow us on Facebook or visit us online at mackids.com.
Our books are friends for life.